PJ Norris and The Town with the Butterfly Problem

PJ NORRIS AND THE TOWN WITH THE BUTTERFLY PROBLEM

FIREWING INVESTIGATIONS BOOK ONE

S. USHER EVANS

Sun's Golden Ray Publishing

PENSACOLA, FL

Cover Design and Chapter Typography by Sun's Golden Ray Publishing
Map Designed by Frederick Kroner with Stardust Book Services
Line Editing by Danielle Fine, By Definition Editing
Proofreading by Lisa Henson, Capitol Editing

Sun's Golden Ray Publishing
Pensacola, FL
www.sgr-pub.com

For ordering information, please visit
www.sgr-pub.com/orders

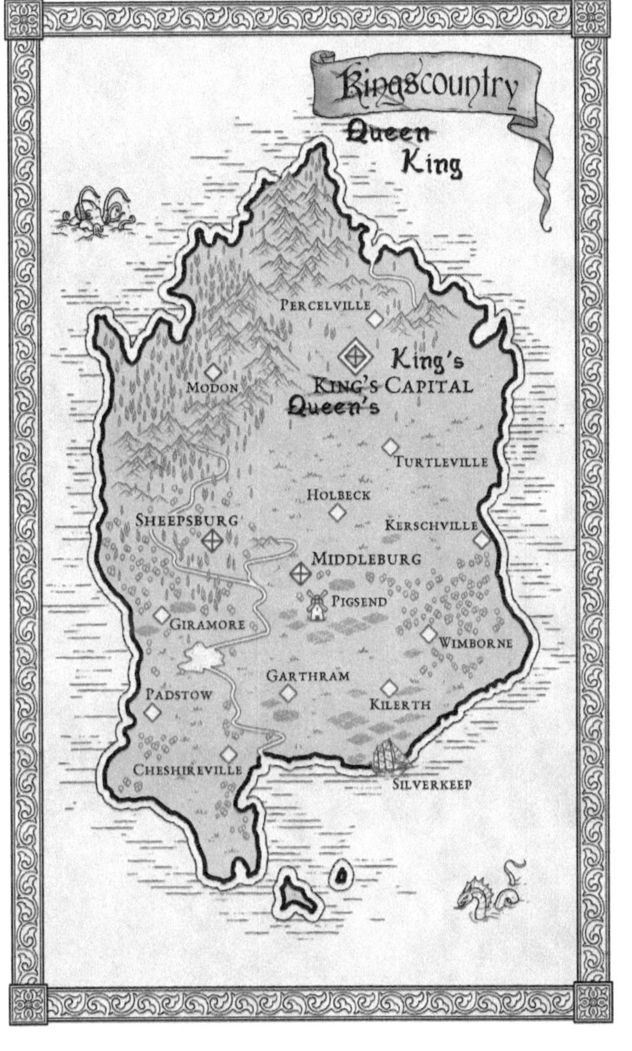

Kingscountry
Queen
King
PERCELVILLE
King's
KING'S CAPITAL
MODON
Queen's
TURTLEVILLE
HOLBECK
SHEEPSBURG
KERSCHVILLE
MIDDLEBURG
PIGSEND
GIRAMORE
WIMBORNE
GARTHRAM
PADSTOW
KILERTH
CHESHIREVILLE
SILVERKEEP

CHAPTER ONE

"Okay. We *probably* shouldn't have mentioned that you're a dragon shifter."

PJ Norris glared at his best friend Grant Hamblin and shouldered his bag as they walked down the empty dirt road. While all was quiet now, the angry shouts of the crowd that had all but chased them from the small town of Timberson still echoed in PJ's ears.

"I'm not the one who opened his big mouth," PJ said.

"Oh, who remembers who said what?"

"I do," PJ said pointedly.

"Well, lesson learned, then, eh? We won't mention it in the next town." Grant, who'd never absorbed a single criticism in his life, just slapped PJ on the shoulder. "Anyway, you didn't really think there was a dragon shifter in that town, did you?"

PJ hoped not. He was exactly two days into a quest to find more of his kind, who had been all but wiped off the map after a magic-hating queen decimated their numbers. He, himself, was just a fluke of blood and circumstances, found by a trio of elderly shifters he affectionately called "the grannies" when he'd been on the brink of his first transformation. Now that the queen was gone, the grannies had passed their task onto PJ, though they'd been a *little* light on the details of how he was to accomplish said task.

To be honest, he had no idea what he was doing. Timberson was only a day's walk from where they'd started in Sheepsburg, and PJ had felt *something* when they'd walked into town, which had prompted him to stay and poke around. But before he'd been able to ask a single question, Grant had wanted to impress a pretty girl with long lashes with the truth about what they were doing there…

…which had led to them being run out of town by an angry mob with pitchforks and torches.

"Well, it's a moot point now," Grant said to PJ's silence. "I mean, I think you really would've *known* it, right? Not just had that wishy-washy feeling. Like, that amulet of yours would've been like, 'there is a big, honkin' dragon somewhere in the vicinity,' right?"

"The grannies didn't know I was there until Bev found me," PJ replied, recalling when the intrepid owner of the Weary Dragon Inn had saved him *and* their beloved town of Pigsend before he trampled it.

"But they knew *someone* was, right? That's why they didn't leave."

PJ pulled the golden amulet from beneath his shirt and inspected it. It was new (to him, at least), a gift from the grannies to help with his task. "I wish they'd have included more in their letter. Even just a mention of which way to go first."

"What'd they say? If you run into trouble, the amulet will give you what you need?" Grant said.

PJ made a noncommittal noise. It certainly hadn't done much in Timberson. But it was a little different than his old amulet, which had muted all traces of magic to almost nonexistence. Now, he felt…something. If he concentrated, he could almost see a pair of red, burning eyes just above his own, scanning the empty forest. He still wasn't sure if that was true or if he was imagining it—and he certainly hadn't mentioned it to Grant.

"Well, I think that town just wasn't the right spot for us to begin our search anyway," Grant said with a nod. "I'm sure the next one will be better."

"As long as you don't tell people what I am," PJ

said.

"Yeah, yeah." He grinned. "So, what do you want to do for dinner? I'm starving."

PJ stopped, staring at his friend incredulously. "Are you joking?"

"No."

He gestured toward the forest. "Where are we gonna get food? I don't see a tavern anywhere around here, do you?"

Grant made a noise. "Well, let's get a move on, then. There's bound to be a town just down the road. It's not as if we'll have to sleep under a tree."

But they kept walking, the light dwindled, and they saw no sign of civilization. Just a long, winding forest. They hadn't even seen a fellow traveler on the road in hours, which made PJ a little leery. Did the locals know something about the forest that they didn't? He glanced down at his amulet, which was once again hidden beneath his dark green tunic. It certainly looked expensive, though if a thief tried to take it off him, they'd have more to contend with than just an angry teenager.

"This stinks." Grant sighed again, sounding a bit morose now. Had he, by some miracle, actually understood that their predicament was his fault? And was he, even more miraculously, feeling *bad* about it?

"Look, it's getting dark," PJ said, unable to

enjoy his friend's misery, even if it was well-deserved. "We should probably set up camp while there's still light."

"Camp?" Grant made a face. "You mean like—"

"Like make a fire, find some water, see if there's some wild berries or mushrooms—"

"Absolutely not."

PJ sighed, looking up at the pink sky. "Then what do you suggest?"

"Didn't the grannies say that amulet would give you what you needed?" Grant asked. "Why don't you ask *it* to find us shelter?"

PJ shook his head. "I shouldn't be wielding magic unless I know what I'm doing."

"Then I'll do it." Grant walked up to PJ and bent down so he was eye-level with the amulet. "Oi! Amulet! Why don't you magic us up some food and water and a pair of sleeping bags?"

"You don't have to yell at it."

Grant straightened, pursing his lips. "This thing's broken."

"Or that's not how it works," PJ said with an exasperated sigh.

"Then how about this?" Grant asked with a mischievous smile. "Take it *off*, turn into a giant thing with wings, then fly us somewhere we can get a hot meal."

PJ pursed his lips at him. "There are *several*

reasons that's an awful idea, not the least of which is I don't know how I got back to this," he gestured toward himself, "form after I shifted the first time." He paused. "Not to mention, I wasn't exactly in my right mind as a dragon that first time, either. So…"

"So?"

"So *you* might be dinner," PJ finished with a knowing smirk.

Grant made a face. "You wouldn't—"

"I wouldn't, but what's to say the dragon feels the same way?" PJ said.

There was a very good chance the dragon knew Grant as much as PJ did and wouldn't consider his best friend a delicious snack. But PJ also wouldn't put it past Grant to take his amulet off in the dead of night, just to see what would happen. So better to put a little fear into Grant, just in case.

"*Fine*," Grant said with a sigh. "Where are we going to sleep then?"

"I see a spot over there next to that tree that looks comfy."

~

PJ hadn't ever had to sleep outside, nor did he have any idea what was edible in this unrecognizable forest, but he did, at least, have the wherewithal to build a small fire and locate a stream to fill their empty canteens. The latter, he suspected, was helped by his dragon eyes, but he didn't share that with

Grant. As the rest of the light disappeared completely, PJ was grateful they'd stopped when they did.

"I'm *hungry*," Grant whined. "Is this worse than having to go back home to Pigsend as failures? At least there's food there. Bev wouldn't let me starve."

"Bev would make you work off your tab, I'm sure," PJ said, sitting back and looking up. Bev was a wonderfully generous person with her time and energy, but she definitely expected payment of some kind for eating her food. "I wonder if my parents got my letter yet. They're going to be so upset to hear we left."

"I'm sure Vicky got mine," Grant said, sounding a bit like he wished she hadn't. "And I'm sure it confirmed everything she suspects about me."

Previously, PJ and Grant had been enrolled at Sheepsburg University, a prestigious learning institution that they'd only gotten accepted to because of Grant's newfound familial wealth and connections. PJ, who had neither money nor knew anyone outside their quaint farming town, had been grateful for the chance, knowing full well he'd only been included to keep an eye on Grant. That had worked fine the first year, but as the second year of courses grew more complex, Grant's grades had fallen—and their paid-for apartment and tuition disappeared.

At that dark moment, PJ had received a letter from his dragon-shifting mentors, along with the amulet, and the duo had set off on a new adventure. He still had the letter, which he pulled from his pack and read for the millionth time by the firelight.

> We won't lie; this isn't an easy assignment. You'll hit many dead ends. In fact, in the seven years we traveled the country, the only shifter we found was you. But we're confident there are more out there, especially now, as more children come of age without the queen's soldiers. Even though magic is legal, it's still not quite as safe as it was before the queen made a mess of things, and of course, a new shifter would need guidance and help as you did when we found you. So if you find one, bring them to the Dragon's Nest (where you had your first shift), and we'll handle it from there.
>
> As you travel, remember that dragon shifts can take many forms, so if something feels off, investigate until you know for sure what it could be. It's now more important than ever to do whatever we can to help our neighbors, to give grace and support where others might find fault, and to turn every stone until the truth comes to light.

A snore echoed from across the fire. Grant clearly hadn't had any problem overcoming his hunger and falling asleep, nor had he had a thought for their safety in this desolate wood. PJ, who was exhausted himself, nestled against the tree and crossed his arms, annoyed that he'd have to take the first shift—

Go sleep. It safe.

PJ sat upright. The voice had reverberated through his body from his head to his toes, echoing between his ears.

"H-hello?" PJ said, looking around, although he knew in his aching bones that sound had come from within.

There was a warmth in his body that hadn't been there earlier, one that felt disturbingly similar to his first shift. But unlike then, when the need had been constant and frantic, the dragon was calm, content, well-rested, and at its leisure.

PJ relaxed, pulling his amulet out and looking at it. Although it was disconcerting to hear voices, it had seemed familiar in a way. Like his father's deep baritone, or the feel of his mother stroking his hair when he was a child. Like it had been a part of him his entire life, only he'd just now noticed it.

"Well, if you're sure," PJ said to the darkness.

The voice didn't answer, but he got the sense that the dragon would keep the watch.

"I'll do my best to sleep then," PJ whispered, adjusting himself against the tree. It was hardly comfortable, but the long day had caught up to him, and he fell into a dreamless slumber.

~

Morning came too early, but PJ was glad to get up and moving. Hunger gnawed at him now, and he practically dragged Grant back onto the road, grateful there was one to follow, at least. But the thought of going a full day without eating left PJ cranky. Grant kept his gripes to a minimum, especially when PJ glared at him for complaining, but the miserable sighs seemed uncontrollable.

PJ distracted himself from the discomfort by searching inward for that strange, familiar voice. He hoped it might speak up to tell them how far until the end of this forest—or if they were destined to wander forever. But although he could feel the dragon, it wasn't as chatty as it had been the night before. Perhaps it was nocturnal.

Finally, the end of the forest was in sight, as the trees opened to more familiar grassy hills and distant farmhouses. Of course, they were nowhere near Pigsend, but at least the terrain seemed less intimidating. Plus, farmhouses meant farmers, and hopefully, *like* Pigsend, the farmers convened in a town to get supplies. Maybe even held a market where they could buy food. Not that they had much coin, but PJ was getting desperate enough to use some of it.

And it seemed he wasn't the only desperate one. When Grant spotted an orchard of apple trees, he immediately hopped the fence.

"Where are you going?" PJ asked.

"Getting food," Grant said, his gaze on the trees and a bit of drool on his lips. "I'm sure they won't miss one apple. Or three. I'm starving."

"No," PJ said, jumping the fence and hurrying over to him. "We aren't thieves."

"I mean, I don't see a town anywhere, do you?" Grant said. "Nor do I see a farmer. Come *onnn*, if they catch us, we can just pay them—"

"No, Grant," PJ said, his voice taking on a deeper tone than he'd intended.

Perhaps the dragon wasn't as nocturnal as he thought. Or maybe he was just really hungry, and his neck ached from sleeping at an odd angle, and it was *quite* annoying to always have to be the mature one and say no when he really *really* wanted—

There was a gurgling sound. "What was that?" PJ asked.

"What was what?" Grant asked.

PJ scanned the countryside. He hadn't been sure what had caught his attention, but something was drawing him off the road toward the orchard.

"I thought you said—" Grant started.

"Hush."

PJ walked with purpose, ignoring the juicy red

apples that hung within arm's reach. The dragon had scented something. It wanted PJ to find whatever it was. *Needed.*

His pulse rose. Had he found a dragon? Already?

Finally, his human ears caught what the dragon had sensed. Someone was crying for help—a young boy. But where?

The sound of rushing water came next, and PJ's measured walk turned into an all-out sprint. He found the water—a deep, fast-moving creek—but where was the boy?

There.

PJ didn't think twice, throwing off his bag and diving headfirst into the water. He paddled and kicked until he collided with something small. Wrapping his arms around the kid, he pushed off the bottom and used all his might to propel them to the surface. As soon as they reached air, the child coughed and spat up water—a good sign. The river was fast, but PJ was strong, and he was able to swim to the edge, grabbing a nearby root.

"How in the *world* did you hear that?" Grant asked, half-eaten red apple in hand.

"Take him," PJ said, thrusting the child at Grant.

Grant tossed the apple aside and reached down to pluck the boy from the water. PJ hoisted himself up onto dry land then ran a hand through his short, dripping hair.

"You okay, kid?" he said, still breathing heavily.

The boy, who couldn't have been older than eight, nodded, though he looked haunted. "I was fishing with my dad," he said, staring at the water as if it could reach up and snatch him. "There was something. I…" He shook his head. "I fell in."

"You're safe now," PJ said, placing a firm hand on his small shoulder, which was shaking. "C'mon, let's go find your dad." He glanced at the river, which was still rushing as if it had very recently seen a deluge. "I'm sure if we follow the river, we'll get you back to him."

The boy didn't wait for them, all but running back the way he'd come from. PJ rose slowly and picked up his sack, which now hung uncomfortably against his wet clothes.

"What was that about?" Grant asked, picking up his apple and dusting it on his clothes. "Was there something about the kid?"

"I don't know," PJ said, not wanting to think about what might've happened to the boy had he not listened to the dragon. "I just know I needed to save him."

"Hm." Grant pulled a second apple from his pocket and took a bite. "Well, suppo' we'd better fi' his dad, get our rewar', and see why the drag'n was so interested in him."

"You're way too comfortable taking things," PJ said with a glare as they started walking back along the river. "After we make sure the kid gets back to his dad, we're going to find the farmer and pay for the apples."

"Yeah, with what—" Grant blinked. "Um. What is *that?*"

PJ looked down at his amulet, which was glowing beneath his shirt. He had the urge to hold out his hand, and in the center of his palm, a single silver coin appeared.

"What the…?" Grant swiped it and inspected it. "Yeah, it's real, all right. Where did it come from? To pay for this apple?"

PJ didn't think so. "I think it's a reward for saving the boy's life."

"Huh." Grant flipped it in the air and caught it. "So that's how the grannies had all that gold to help out when you shifted back in Pigsend. Every time you knocked down a house, they'd rebuild it and get a few coins?"

"Maybe." They'd never mentioned it to PJ, but it did make sense. They certainly hadn't carried many coins on them. "In any case, we're about to lose the kid, so let's get after him. Maybe he can show us the way to town."

"And give us more money, too."

"Grant…"

CHAPTER TWO

It didn't take long to catch up with the kid, who, despite being saved by PJ, seemed leery of the two teens following him. He didn't answer any of their questions about his name, or where he lived, or any of that. PJ could understand his hesitation.

"Benny?" A man's voice called out moments before a tall, lanky figure appeared around a large tree. "Benny! Oh, thank goodness!"

The boy put on a burst of speed and crashed into his father's arms, breaking into tears.

The man held his son tightly and wordlessly. Then, after a moment, he noticed Grant and PJ—specifically that PJ was drenched. "Did you…?" The man looked down at his son. "You saved his life?"

"Yeah." PJ rubbed the back of his neck. "He said you two were fishing, and—"

"Don't tell your mother," the man said, putting the boy down. "She'll have my head. Least of all because you were skipping school." He turned to PJ and Grant with a kind smile. "Thank you so much. I can't even begin to tell you… My heart still hasn't slowed down since he fell in."

PJ hid a smile. "Well, he seems all right now."

"Just lucky we were passing through when we did," Grant said, giving PJ a meaningful look. "And that we can swim, too!"

But the man didn't seem to catch what Grant was insinuating, inspecting his son as if making sure he truly was all right. As he did so, PJ scrutinized the boy. He certainly didn't *feel* magical, and the dragon was being awfully quiet about him now. Had it only wanted PJ to save a life? That wasn't a *bad* thing. But it didn't seem like the sort of thing a dragon shifter should do regularly.

"In any case, probably should avoid fishing for a couple of days until the river calms down," PJ continued, clearing his throat. "It's pretty fast right now. My dad always told me to avoid playing near Pigsend Creek after a good rain—"

"Pigsend?" Benny's father did a double-take. "You two grew up in Pigsend?"

"*You* know Pigsend?" Grant asked.

"We got caught there in a nasty snowstorm a couple years ago during the winter solstice, had to stay at the Weary Dragon a few nights."

"Oh, I remember that solstice," PJ said with a nod. It was the one right before he'd had his shift, and it had snowed for a week straight. "So you know Bev?"

"I *love* Bev," Benny's father said with a grin. All at once, his hesitation melted away, and he held out his hand. "Byron Werst, at your service. This is my son, Benny. We live in the town of Gilramore, just twenty minutes from here."

PJ shook his hand, relief washing over him. "We've been looking for a town. Been walking through the forest from Timberson the past day or so, and we'd become convinced the forest didn't have an end."

"Yeah, that's quite a walk," Byron said with a nod. "You two must be starving. C'mon, we've got plenty of room at our dinner table, as long as you don't mind a mess of children." He beamed. "You can tell me all about how Bev's doing at the Weary Dragon on the way back."

PJ was glad to share all he knew about Bev, which wasn't much. The innkeeper had been gone for a few months right around the time the queen had fallen but had returned and resumed her life at the Weary Dragon without much of a fuss. PJ had theories about where she'd gone and why but didn't share them.

"Yeah, we were on our way to see my in-laws on the other side of the country," Byron said, as Benny skipped ahead to pick up rocks and throw them. "It started snowing then just wouldn't stop. My wife Abigail was beside herself, but we made it to her parents' a few days late. The kids had a blast at the Weary Dragon, though. Bev was so kind to them, and we'll never forget that. Though we decided we'd never travel during the winter solstice again."

"I don't blame you," PJ said. "But Pigsend is pleasant in the fall, especially during the Harvest Festival. If you're ever wanting to go back."

"I would, but my wife's up to her ears sorting through the mess that the king's inflicted on us," Byron said with a shake of his head.

"What kind of mess?" PJ asked.

"Well, showing up out of the blue, not being dead and overthrowing the queen," Byron said. "Gilramore was one of her first strongholds, and we've really been going through it since word hit us that we no longer work for her." He squinted and tilted his head to the side. "Well, let's just say the queen's strict policies and procedures have all gone up in flames—literally."

"So you worked for the queen?" PJ asked.

He nodded. "I was a registrar."

"What's that?" Grant asked.

"Oh, you boys were probably too young to remember right after the first war," Byron said with a knowing nod. "Well, back when that ended and Her Majesty took control, she wanted to move into peace as quickly as possible. So she ordered a bureau of the registrar to be set up that would keep sworn loyalty statements from former kingside soldiers. Registrars like me kept the loyalty statements up-to-date and checked in on the kingside soldiers about once a year. Made sure they were acclimating to the new normal, not causing trouble, that sort of thing."

The way Byron made it sound, he'd been doing the kingside soldiers a favor. PJ could only imagine a queen-hating soldier like Vellora Witzel, the towering butcher who lived across the street from Bev, willingly submitting herself to yearly updates.

"And they took well to that?" Grant asked, sounding as dubious as PJ felt.

"I mean… They could sign the loyalty pledge, or…" He glanced at his son, who had wandered ahead of them, but not too far that he wasn't listening. "Well. I think you can guess the alternatives. Gilramore was named the regional registrar center for everyone on this side of the country. My wife was the head registrar and had at least a hundred folks working for her."

"All in Gilramore?" PJ asked.

"Spread out over the region," Byron replied. "Gilramore itself isn't that big. Maybe two hundred people. But everyone was employed by the queen."

PJ shared a look with Grant. Definitely should keep mum about the dragon stuff around Byron and his wife. Somehow, he got the feeling their reception in Timberson wouldn't hold a candle to the treatment they'd get here if they found out what PJ really was.

Gilramore came into view, and while it was different, the dirt streets, small cottages with quaint gardens, and kindly people reminded PJ of home. Until, of course, he noticed all the flags and signs and paintings supporting the queen. Not to mention a pair of soldiers still wearing her colors. PJ, who'd run into his fair share of soldiers in Pigsend, tried to avoid looking them in the eye as they walked by, even though they technically had no authority to arrest him. But he'd learned that out in the countryside, rules weren't always followed exactly.

There was a small farmers' market in the center of town, which was full of produce of every color and variety, including the same apples Grant had helped himself to earlier. Around the square, there was also a blacksmith shop, a library, a schoolhouse, the town hall (which was much smaller than Pigsend's), and a collection of offices that bore the queen's symbol.

"That's where Abigail works," Byron said. "Well, used to. Her office is still there, but she spends most of the time at the mayor's office."

"All right there, Byron?"

PJ stopped, staring at one of the soldiers still in uniform. He eyed PJ and Grant suspiciously, and PJ forced himself to meet the soldier's gaze.

"Yeah, just found a couple of friends on the road," Byron said with a smile, patting PJ on the back. "Passing through town."

"Mm." The soldier didn't quite relax all the way. "Lots of that happening these days. Random people just passing through."

"Is that a problem?" Grant asked, crossing his arms and showing none of the fear PJ felt.

"Of course it isn't," Byron said with a laugh. "Ease up, Quentin. I promise, they're not in town to cause trouble. I wouldn't be inviting them to dinner if they were."

Quentin made a face but didn't say anything else, and Byron quickly ushered them onward.

"Who was that?" PJ asked. "And why is he still wearing a uniform?"

"Quentin Shellman. Former queen's soldier." He cleared his throat and made sure they were out of earshot. "I'm not sure Quentin owns any other clothes. He took great pride in working for the queen. He'd just been assigned here from Queen's Capital when it all happened." He shuddered. "Probably for the best. Can't imagine where he'd be after those magical usurpers got their hands on the likes of him. I hear they really did a number on poor Dag Flanigan."

PJ's blood ran cold. Dag Flanigan was a dangerous magic-hunter who'd nearly captured him as he was going through his first shift. It was only thanks to Grant and their other friend Valta Climber that PJ had been able to escape.

"You don't say?" Grant said to cover PJ's silence.

"They let him live, at least, which is..." Byron cleared his throat, glancing down at Benny, who was looking up at his father with wide eyes. "Let's just say the folks in Queen's Capital weren't all so fortunate."

"It's a lovely town," Grant said, perhaps, like PJ, hoping to change the subject away from the figure who'd haunted PJ's nightmares. "Lots of friendly faces." A blacksmith walked by, giving them a once-over as if they'd done something to offend him. "And clearly trusting of newcomers."

"It's not their fault," Byron said. "Ever since... well, things *changed*, there've been more people passing through town. We always had people coming and going, you know, especially at the inn. But they were always associated with the queen."

He pointed to a white building with a thatched roof that seemed similar to the Weary Dragon but instead had a placard describing it as the Gilramore Inn.

"Lately, there've only been strange folks with…" He cleared his throat. "Magic."

"Gotta be careful of those magical folks," Grant said with a solemn nod. "Never know who might be hiding the power to turn into a giant dragon."

PJ could've burned him alive with a glare.

But Byron didn't seem to notice. "I can't even imagine. The inn's resorted to testing people when they come through the door. Not much they can do about it, but we can make them feel unwelcome enough to get the message across. And it's not as if the majority of us have anything better to do."

PJ nodded. There were lots of people out and about, and not a whole lot of people working. What *did* happen to a town employed to enforce the queen's vast network of policies and procedures when those edicts no longer applied? Suppose there were a lot, like Byron, with time on their hands.

Just how much time the former registrar had was evident when he led them to a quaint two-story house on the outskirts of town. The fence had been freshly painted, and based on the overturned dirt, there'd been a slew of new flowers planted recently. The porch was spotless, and also newly painted, and every one of the windows glimmered as if they'd just been washed that morning.

"You have a lovely home," PJ said as they climbed the steps. "I can tell you take a lot of pride in it."

"I don't like sitting still," Byron said. "I spent the last few years traveling the region almost every week. Then all of a sudden, I'm unemployed. Abigail told me I'd better figure out something to do else she'd make me sleep in the barn. So I've been keeping myself busy sprucing up the house."

"And breaking your son out of school?" Grant said.

"Yeah." Byron rubbed the back of his head. "I mean, it was such a nice day. Too nice to be stuck indoors."

"We won't say a word," PJ said.

Benny ran upstairs to get changed, and PJ, whose clothes had mostly dried on the walk back to town, took a seat with Grant in the kitchen. Byron returned from the root cellar with an armful of vegetables to join a cut of bright red beef that had been wrapped in paper.

"We used to eat a lot at the local tavern, but now that I'm out of work, I've got time to really work on my cooking and baking. I've gotten pretty good, I'll tell ya, but I still haven't quite figured out how Bev made that rosemary bread so good."

"I tried once before, too," PJ said. "I think she's just got the magic touch."

"Hopefully not *magic* touch," Byron said with a frown.

"Erm. Figure of speech." PJ shrugged. "I'm fairly sure Bev's normal. Other than her penchant for fixing problems in Pigsend." Grant nudged PJ's foot, and PJ cleared his throat. "So what's going to happen to everyone who was employed by the queen?"

"Frankly, we haven't a clue. The kingside folks have never been known for their *communication*, you know? Right now, everyone's kind of on their own. Some towns are reverting to the way things were, but I can't see us taking down our banners and colors unless we're forced to." He brightened, clearly ready to talk about something else. ""So, you boys said you came from Timberson? What brought you up there?"

"Traveling the country," Grant said before PJ could respond. "We were at the university in Sheepsburg but decided it wasn't for us. Trying to make our fortunes elsewhere, you know? The world's changed, as you said, and there's gotta be opportunity for two bright young men with a hunger to improve themselves. PJ and I have a specific set of skills that I felt were better used helping people in the wider world than learning how business works in a classroom." He flashed a cheeky grin. "It was a good thing we walked by the river when we did."

"You aren't joking." Byron let out a low breath. "To be honest, I'm not sure how I'm going to explain you two to my wife without telling her the *whole* story."

"Well, if you're worried—" Grant began, but this time, PJ was faster.

"We promise we won't say a word about it," he said, giving Grant a warning glance. Better to ask nicely than threaten him with blackmail. "We'll be content to get a hot meal and learn a little more about the town."

"And maybe a place to sleep?" Grant managed.

"That might be a bridge too far to ask my wife," Byron said, rubbing his chin thoughtfully. "But you know, the only thing she can say is no. Either way, we'll figure something out. There really is no way I can repay you two for what you did today."

"We were happy to help," PJ said, picking up a knife. "Shall I help you with those potatoes? And Grant can peel those carrots, too."

Grant was not pleased to be volunteered to help but thankfully kept his comments to himself. PJ worked diligently on the spuds, waiting for the right time to talk with Grant about everything, but Byron wasn't gone long enough for PJ to get more than a hasty reminder to stop acting like a grifter. After all, they'd found a place to eat, and maybe to sleep for the night—PJ wasn't about to let Grant ruin *this*, too.

Not long after they started on the vegetables, Abigail and two other kids (Pascal, age six, and little Margo, age three) arrived, and she was less than pleased to see two strangers in her kitchen. Byron, of course, didn't mention that they'd saved Benny's life, perhaps hoping that the shared connection to Pigsend would loosen the frown on her face.

"While we did have a lovely, if *extended,* stay in Pigsend, I'm not sure that means we can host two boys who just happened to live there," Abigail said, giving her husband a death glare. "Just because, Byron?"

"Well, erm…" Byron shifted uncomfortably, clearly torn between helping them and not wanting to get himself in trouble.

"Look, I understand," PJ said, standing upright. "How about this? We can earn our keep another way? Do you have a horse in the back? My parents are farriers, so I've been doing that since I could walk, practically. We'd be happy to reshoe her in exchange for a plate of dinner."

"We do," Abigail said quietly, shooting her husband a look that could've killed him. "Byron was supposed to re-shoe her last week, but—" She sighed. "Yes, I suppose that could work. There are some tools in the barn for you to use."

"Great," PJ said, rising and nodding for Grant to follow him. The two teens quickly escaped, with PJ making a beeline to the barn and Grant walking a lot slower.

"Peej, I know you got a fuzzy feeling about that kid, but…" He turned to look back at the house, and, presumably, the town beyond. "These folks look serious about anti-magic stuff."

"All the more reason for us to stay," PJ said. "Can you imagine a dragon shifter coming into their power here?"

"I don't think they'd get farther than their first puff of smoke," Grant said. "Fine. We'll stay. But I say we use that silver we earned saving his life to get a room at that lovely inn—"

"The one where they test people for magic before letting them in?" PJ asked with a quirked brow.

"They can test me, and you can sneak in a window," Grant said, throwing his arms up. "But at least we can have a hot meal without being glared at. That Abigail looked at us like we were a pair of criminals. She's not going to let us sleep in her house. We'll be lucky if she doesn't call that soldier on us."

"We just need to keep our heads down until I can get to know the kid a little better," PJ said. "Or I can figure out why the dragon wanted me to save him."

"*The dragon* wanted you to save him?" Grant asked, giving him a sideways glance. "What's that supposed to mean?"

PJ shrugged, not sure he wanted to share exactly what was going on until he understood it better himself. He opened the latch to the horse's stall and let himself in. The old mare gave him a suspicious *neigh*, so PJ held out his hand in peace, as his parents had taught him. Eventually, the horse came over to investigate, sniffing him, then allowed him to pat her on the nose.

"That's a good girl," PJ whispered. "I'm just here to check your shoes, if that's all right?"

"So you're talking to horses now, too?" Grant crossed his arms and leaned against the doorframe. "What else are you hiding from me?"

"I'm not talking to horses." PJ sighed as he checked the horse's feet. The shoes were actually fine, in his estimation, but a hoof cleaning was overdue. "I mean, no more than I did before. They don't answer."

"So what's the deal with the dragon, eh? Is it talking to you? I thought you said it was just a sense."

"It was a sense. Is a sense." PJ found the cleaning equipment in a small closet. The tools were a little rusted, but they'd do the trick—and thankfully, they had wooden handles, so he wouldn't have to touch the iron. "But it actually spoke to me last night."

"Really?" Grant quirked a brow. "Are you sure you weren't just hearing things?"

"It's hard to explain," PJ said. "But I need you to trust me—"

"I do trust you," Grant said. "But I also gotta look out for you. And maybe your dragon just wanted you to earn a nice silver coin for saving that kid then move on. I can't imagine it could've predicted we'd land in a staunchly anti-magic town in a house full of high-ranking queen-lovers." He took a step toward PJ. "This place ain't safe for you, Peej."

"If it's not safe for me, it wouldn't be safe for Benny, if he turned out to be something else. Besides that, nobody will know what I am unless you open your big mouth again," PJ said with a glare.

"I'm not saying *anything*."

"Then what was that quip about dragon shifters?" PJ said.

"Just putting him at ease," Grant said, as if that were obvious. "If I told him you weren't a dragon shifter, he might think you were one."

PJ stared at the roof of the barn for a moment to gather his patience. "In *any* case, I do get the sense the Wersts are good people. Maybe have some funny ideas, but that's probably just the way they were raised. I'm sure they thought the queen was doing the right thing by making the world safer. Byron said they treated the soldiers they managed with respect, you know? I think that says a lot."

Grant sniffed. "Yeah, I get the sense this town

might not be full of kindly folk like Byron. I'd much rather just get our food and move on." He sighed. "But you're the—"

"Ssh." The hair rose on PJ's neck as he put his finger to his mouth.

A moment later, Byron appeared, looking somewhat sheepish. "So hey." He coughed, not meeting their gazes. "Thanks again for—"

"Saving your son?" Grant said pointedly.

"Yes, that, and not telling Abigail about it," he said, looking at the ground as if he'd just had the worst haranguing of his life. "She's been on edge since the queen fell." He sighed. "Look, she said you can stay for dinner, but she put her foot down about you two sleeping in the house."

"What about the barn?" PJ said, before Grant could argue. "Would she mind if we slept in the hayloft?"

Byron made a face. "You'd rather sleep—"

"It's much better than last night," PJ said. "If that's all right with her. You won't even notice we're here. I think we might be staying in town a few days after all."

"Really?" Byron frowned more. "Erm…"

"Once we get our bearings, we'll find different accommodations," PJ added quickly. "But just for tonight—"

"Yeah, I'm sure she won't mind that," Byron

said, exhaling. "And, erm, thanks again for not ratting me out. I know it makes it harder to justify you sleeping here, but—" He swallowed. "She really would *kill* me."

"Don't worry about it," PJ said, waving him off. "We all have secrets."

PJ had forgotten how hungry he was until Byron put a full plate of meat and vegetables in front of him. He all but inhaled the food, grateful for every morsel. The Wersts had a full table, with all five family members, PJ, Grant, and Byron's sister Mary, who also regarded the boys with the same level of mistrust as Abigail. Even with the tension in the air between the adults, the children provided lots of entertainment and activity, with Benny and Pascal leading the lion's share of the conversation and sweet Margo popping up to add more context. To their credit, neither Werst boy let slip their father had taken the eldest out of school or what had transpired, which to PJ was the mark of a very loyal boy indeed.

Throughout dinner, PJ couldn't help but observe the eldest boy, searching for *anything* amiss and came up empty. Had it really just been because the boy needed saving?

I really should write to the grannies again.

But the grannies were presumably enjoying their

retirement in the mountains, and PJ felt strange about bothering them when they hadn't been retired for a week yet. No, he'd figure this one out on his own.

"So, Sheepsburg, hm?" Mary asked, breaking PJ's attention away from Benny. "That's quite the university. How did a pair of boys from a farming town get accepted there?"

"Funny story," Grant said, putting down his knife and fork as he grinned at PJ.

"Settle in, folks," PJ drawled, sitting back. "This is his *favorite* thing to tell."

"That's because it's so good," Grant said with a cheeky smile. "So it all begins with my sister Vicky and me, growing up as poor orphans in Pigsend. Our mother was from a hoity-toity family in Sheepsburg, but we thought she'd been disowned and didn't get her inheritance, on account of she married our father, who was a nobody and ran off to fight in the war—"

"Kingside or queenside?" Abigail interrupted.

"Queenside, obviously," Grant said, though PJ wasn't sure if that was true—especially as his uncle had turned out to be a high-ranking soldier to the king. "In any case, Vic and I never saw a silver of this great fortune growing up, even after our mother died and our father...went off to bravely fight for Her Majesty. My sister was only sixteen, but she taught herself to sew and became a seamstress to support us both." He put his hand over his heart. "What a gem she was. Suffered mightily to give us both a good life."

PJ had to resist a snort, knowing that while Vicky was "suffering," Grant was goofing off and talking back to her.

"Well, a few years ago, she gets engaged to Allen —you probably met him. His bakery was across the street from the Weary Dragon," Grant said, and both the Wersts nodded. "Anyway, she invites our two aunts to town for the wedding. Then stuff starts happening, you know? The flowers she'd put into bouquets were salted instead of fed, the wine she ordered was all spoiled, her *dress* caught fire, the cake fell over—"

"Goodness me." Abigail straightened, looking at Byron as if this were the worst thing she'd ever heard. "Your poor sister!"

"Poor sister is right," Grant said with an emphatic nod. "Because we find out Vicky's actually about to get that inheritance once she marries Allen. And someone had cursed her to make sure she didn't."

Both Abigail and Mary gasped, grabbing each other's hands. "No!"

"Yeah," Grant said with a laugh. "Turns out, there was a stipulation that Vicky's part of our mother's inheritance would come to us if Vicky married before a certain age. But the one who knew that was our Aunt Lucy. So she'd bought a curse of some kind or another, put it on a bracelet she'd given to Vic, and that caused all the nonsense. Well, my other aunt Marion decided *that* wasn't fair, so she and Vicky got it all sorted out."

"I do hope someone reported her to Her Majesty's authorities," Mary said with a frown.

"Actually, Allen's father is… Gosh, what's his name?" Grant rubbed the back of his head. "Zack Mackey?

"*Zed* Mackey?" Abigail gasped. "*The* Zed Mackey? The queenside soldier?"

"That's the one." Grant sat back, smirking like he'd just secured himself and PJ a spot indoors this evening. "Anyway, he was around for the wedding and handled her."

"Did your sister marry Allen in the end?" Abigail asked.

"Nah." Grant shook his head, and when Abigail frowned, he added, "It's for the best. They were awful to each other. Vicky's much happier now."

"How did you end up in Sheepsburg, then?" Mary asked.

"After all that happened, Vic wanted a change of pace, and our other aunt Marion offered to have her and me move to Sheepsburg to be closer to family as they sorted through the inheritance stuff."

"Vicky was very generous to offer to pay my tuition as well," PJ said. "And my parents told me if I didn't take her up on it, they'd disown *me*."

"So why'd you leave the university, then?" Mary asked, staring at them as if she knew the answer.

"Well, after a few years, we both agreed our talents were better spent out in the world helping people," Grant said, flashing a look at Byron. "So that's how we ended up here. Helping."

"No one needs helping here, unless you can put Her Majesty back on her throne," Abigail said with a sniff. "I mean, clearly your aunt was in no position to be wielding magic. Imagine, spending all that time putting together a wedding like that, only to have it fall apart because someone has a vendetta against you."

"Hear, hear," Mary said with a firm nod.

"You folks don't have any oddities?" Grant asked. "Barns collapsing? Weird fires? People acting shifty?"

PJ had to close his eyes so they wouldn't see him roll them. *So much for subtlety.*

"Not in the least," Abigail said, her tone changing from interested to cool in the blink of an eye as she rose. "We are an upstanding town, one of Her Majesty's shining examples of cooperation and loyalty." She looked down at the plate. "At least, we were."

"Why don't Grant and I tackle the dishes?" PJ said, hoping to salvage the conversation before it went any further south.

"No, that's fine. It's getting late, and the children need to go to bed. I'd prefer it if you'd…" She glanced at her husband.

"Of course," PJ said, rising. "C'mon, Grant, let's give them their evening."

The horse, at least, was happy to see them, especially as PJ had grabbed an apple from the stash in the pantry to feed her. Then they climbed up to the loft, which was a little warmer than sleeping outside under a tree, and made their beds.

"Well, this is *so* much nicer than the inn," Grant said, fluffing up a pile of hay. "We really can't use our money to sleep in a *real* bed?" He scoffed. "I seriously thought my curse story would've worked on her."

"It probably works better when you're not in a town full of people who hate magic," PJ said, lying down and yawning.

"It never used to matter," Grant replied. "People love a good redemption arc." He sighed. "So what do you think? Any more conversation from that dragon? Should we move on or stick around to see what's up?"

PJ put his hand over his amulet. His own heart was uncertain, but the feeling in his mind seemed content to stay. There was something amiss in this town—perhaps not with the Wersts themselves, but something else.

Stay.

PJ sat up, looking at Grant. "Did you hear that?"

"Hear what?"

PJ shivered. That answered that. "We stay."

"Then I suggest we go back down to the river and look for more drowning kids, because I'm *not* going to sleep in a hayloft two days in a row."

The hay wasn't quite as comfortable as PJ had hoped, but at least they'd had shelter from the rainstorm that passed through overnight. As they rose and removed straw from their hair, Grant glanced out the large opening toward the small house.

"Do you think Abigail's gonna feed us breakfast or are we on our own?" he asked with a sniff.

PJ sighed, reaching into his bag to count their meager coins. On the whole, he wasn't really keen on spending any of it, especially as there wasn't a guarantee when they'd get more from the amulet. Despite Grant's desire to sit by the river, PJ doubted young boys fell in all that often.

"I'm sure the farmers' market is open already," he said. "But first we need to thank our hosts."

"I wouldn't call them *hosts*," Grant muttered, pulling another piece of hay from his shirt.

"They fed us and put a roof over our heads," PJ said. "You've really got to learn how to be grateful, you know that? Things could *always* be worse."

"You go talk with them, then." Grant snatched one of the silvers out of PJ's hand. "I'll find us some breakfast."

PJ didn't love that they were splitting up—Grant's mouth had gotten them in trouble the last time that happened—but he also didn't think Grant could hide his disdain, so PJ let him leave. He tended to the horse, making sure she had fresh hay and water and found her another apple in the stores.

"Glad you got something to eat this morning," PJ said, stroking her nose. "Now, tell me the truth, is there anything strange happening in this town, or am I just losing it?"

The horse let out a loud breath.

"Great, thanks," PJ muttered.

"Why are you talking to the horse?" Benny stood at the front door of the barn, his hair freshly wet and combed and a bag slung around his shoulder.

"Hey, there." PJ peered behind him to see if his

parents were around. "Where are your folks?"

"They're back at the house. They thought I went to school already, but I wanted to..." He puffed out his chest. "Wanted to thank you for yesterday."

"Happy to help," PJ said, turning to examine the boy one final time. He was starting to wonder if he'd imagined the whole thing the day before. "Listen, I wanted to ask you something. Have you noticed anything strange about yourself lately?"

Benny frowned. "What do you mean?"

PJ decided to come right out with it. "Like you feel there's something inside you that wants to come out? Something that feels on fire, almost? Maybe you've woken up to burnt bedsheets or—"

Benny's eyes widened. "Is *that* what my mom was talking about? She said I'd just get chest hair!"

PJ laughed. "No, that's not... I mean, yeah, that might happen one day, but I'm talking about..." He walked up to Benny, who was about at chest-level. "There's nothing magical happening to you?"

Benny made a face. "Magic is wrong, my mom says."

"Yeah, but sometimes people..." PJ placed a hand on the kid's shoulder. Nothing—absolutely nothing—came up. "Never mind. Forget I said anything. You run along to school. I don't want your mom thinking I had a hand in turning you into a delinquent, all right?"

"My dad's got that handled," Benny said, adjusting his books on his shoulder with a smirk. "Are you staying for dinner again?"

"I don't know," PJ said. "But I'll be sure to find you and say goodbye if we do leave."

"Benjamin Byron Werst, I *know* I don't see you hanging around after you're supposed to be at school." Abigail's voice rang out from the yard.

Benny yelped and scrambled out of the barn, and PJ had to laugh. There was something comforting about this family that made him homesick for his own parents. He walked into the yard to find Abigail standing on the back steps of the house, her lips pursed and her whole body tense.

PJ walked up to her anyway and clasped his hands behind his back. "Erm. I wanted to thank you," PJ said, plastering on his nicest, most generous smile. "For dinner last night and for letting us stay in the hayloft."

"You're moving on, then?" she asked, almost hopefully.

"Not quite yet," he said. "But we'll be sure to find alternate lodgings tonight." He nodded toward the stable. "I did get your horse all fixed up. Her shoes looked fine, but I gave her hooves a good cleaning. She's got water and hay, too. She's a sweet girl. Let me work on her without a single complaint." He paused. "Benny came by to… Well,

I'm not sure why he came by."

Abigail relaxed a little. "Because he thinks you're the most fascinating person he's ever seen." She smiled and nodded back toward the house. "I'm not sure what you did to impress him, but he's your biggest fan. They were aghast we made you sleep in the loft last night, in fact. Benny wouldn't stop asking me to have you stay for dinner again."

"He's a good kid," PJ said.

She hopped from one foot to the other. "How long did you say you were staying in town?"

"I'm honestly not sure," PJ said, wishing his dragon would be a *bit* more communicative. Benny was clearly not the reason, so why did the dragon want them to stick around? "I hope we find out today." He nodded. "Thank you again for your hospitality."

"You know, it really wasn't that much of a bother to have you two sleeping in the hayloft," she said, leaning on the doorframe. "And Byron said you were so helpful with getting dinner ready, too. Seems Bev taught you a thing or two."

"I did help her out for a couple of weeks," he said. "But don't ask me to make bread. Could never get the hang of it."

She smiled. "Well, if you are still in town this evening, feel free to come by for a plate. And you're welcome to our hayloft as long as you need it."

"You hypnotized her," Grant said when PJ told him about the conversation with Abigail. He'd been unsuccessful finding breakfast—the farmers' market hadn't started yet, and the inn didn't serve it either—so he'd been loitering near the town hall steps waiting for PJ.

"I don't think that's one of my abilities," PJ said, looking around. "And maybe quiet down on the discussion about *that*, will you?"

"How else do you explain her hating us yesterday and liking us today?" Grant asked, leaning back on the stair and closing his eyes.

"Gratitude and humility," PJ said. "Things you really should brush up on."

He scoffed. "So what's the plan today, boss?"

PJ sat next to his friend. "I honestly don't know. I hate to just sit around and wait for something to happen, but I kind of feel like that's what I'm supposed to do." He shrugged, watching the farmers as they rolled into town on wagons laden with fruit and other produce. "Get to know some more folks, too."

"That seems like a lot of wasted energy since we aren't going to stay here very long."

A shadow fell over them as Quentin stood before them, wearing the same uniform as well as a scowl that made it clear the boys were most unwelcome in Gilramore. He shifted so his sword glinted in the sunlight, and PJ wondered if he'd ever *actually* used it or just wore it for show.

"You're still here?" he asked, looming over them with a menacing glare.

"No, we're ghosts," Grant replied with a hearty roll of his eyes. "Of course we're still here. Where else would we be?"

"In a town that puts up with miscreants and gangs." He thumbed his nose. "What do you want with the Wersts?"

"We have mutual friends," PJ said. "They invited us to dinner and to stay the night."

"And what's your business in Gilramore?"

That, PJ didn't have a good answer to—but Grant spoke up before he could. "We're here to investigate a magical disturbance."

"Are we?" PJ said, casting a sideways glance at him. *What is he thinking?*

"There are no magical disturbances," he said, narrowing his gaze.

"Aren't there?" Grant leaned back on his palms. "Lots of magical people criss-crossing the countryside lately, aren't there? They like to stop in towns like this, cause a little trouble. Or, people who've been hiding their magic all this time, they're ready to show off a bit. Take some revenge. Peej and I travel from town to town helping them figure out what's causing the barns to implode and fires to mysteriously start. Then we make sure that magical culprit sees justice."

PJ stared at him, unable to make a sound.

"Oh, yeah?" Quentin crossed his arms over his chest. "And what kinda *magical problems* are you here to solve? Because no one in Gilramore has a lick of magic. And if they did, we'd make sure they'd be run out of town."

"Our magic-hunting skills led us here," Grant said. "We were trained by the great Dag Flanigan, you know."

PJ had to bite his cheek to keep from reacting, but he still turned to Grant with a *what are you doing* sort of look.

"Dag Flanigan, eh? Taught *you*?" Quentin sniffed. "You don't look the type."

"I mean, we don't work for him anymore, obviously," Grant said. "So we're...sort of freelancers."

"Are you now?"

"Yeah," Grant continued, pausing to think for a moment. "We set up our own shop. We're called Firewing Investigations."

"Firewing Investigations?" PJ and Quentin said at the same time.

"Yeah." Grant smirked. "It's a combination of our last names, you know?"

"*What* my friend is trying to say is that we're not here to cause trouble," PJ said, finally unsticking his tongue from the roof of his mouth. "And we hope to find nothing of interest here, so we can move on by this afternoon."

"Hm." Quentin shifted his tunic. "Well, if you *do* discover anything, you can bring it to my attention. We don't exactly have a sheriff anymore, but I've been serving as our law enforcement until the idiots in *Queen's*—because I ain't calling it by the other name—Capital get their act together and send someone else."

PJ nodded. "We'll be happy to do that."

Quentin sauntered away, and somehow the uppity soldier actually looked like he believed them. PJ turned to Grant, who was smirking like the cat who finally caught the canary, and kicked him hard in the shoe.

"*What is wrong with you?*" PJ said through clenched teeth. "Firewing Investigations? Trained by Dag Flanigan? Are you *trying* to get us—?"

"What? Arrested?" He sniffed. "Look, Flanigan's long gone, but clearly, everyone in town knows who he is, right? So we can fib a little bit, as long as it gets Soldier Too-Big-For-His-Britches off our backs for a few hours. And besides that, it's not a *complete* lie. We are here investigating magical issues, *should* they arise." He shrugged. "If you ask me, Peej, you should be applauding my quick wit and ability to think on my feet."

PJ wasn't about to do that, lest his friend's head grow too large for his body to carry, so instead he sat next to him. "Well, something magical had better happen quickly."

"Then I'm sure a barn's collapsing *right now*, and we'll hear about it momentarily."

There was no barn collapse nor anything else of interest for the next three hours. PJ and Grant loitered on the front steps of the town hall until the marble stairs became too hard, then they wandered the farmers' market. PJ purchased a bushel of apples for their silver, which Grant was horrified to learn would go to their hosts as a thank-you gift.

"For sleeping in a barn?" he said.

"And feeding us," PJ reminded him.

"We did save their son," Grant shot back.

PJ didn't want to argue, so he just moved on to the next booth, examining the potatoes and other root vegetables, though he had no interest in buying them. The farmers, at least, were a little friendlier than the soldiers, but when PJ asked if they'd seen anything strange or out of the ordinary, none of them had anything to report.

"Only thing strange is that there are a bunch of queen's soldiers loitering around with too much time on their hands," said one of the farmers, a short woman named Ygritte, who had with long braids and dark brown skin. She pointed to a group of soldiers who'd taken PJ and Grant's spot on the town square steps and, from the loudness and rudeness of their conversation, seemed to have little care for the schoolhouse next door.

"I'm sure it hasn't been easy for them," PJ said, trying to sound neutral. "I wonder what they'll do from now on? Can't be a role for registrars now that the queen is gone."

"If they had any sense," the farmer next to her, named Orville, said, "that lot would go into hiding. They've got a few hundred kingside soldiers who would leap at the chance to get revenge."

"Really?" PJ frowned. "What'd they do?"

"I don't know the details, myself," Ygritte said. "But you hear things. People saying they were faking records. Making the kingside soldiers pay 'em an extra gold or two to sign their documents to say they weren't getting into trouble. But it could just be rumors, you know." She busied herself with adjusting the crates of produce on her stand. "Don't want them coming over here to cause trouble."

"I won't say a word," PJ said with a smile. "Thank you for your time."

"I overheard you telling Quentin you were in Dag Flanigan's regiment," she said. "And you're in town to help with magical problems. Did someone send for you?"

"Should they have?" PJ asked.

Ygritte shook her head. "No. Just wondering why you thought Gilramore was a good place to stop. We haven't had a lick of magic in years. No trouble, either, not with all the soldiers who moved to town."

PJ smiled. "Well, so far, it looks like our information about this place might've been incorrect. I think we'll stay one more night then move on in the morning. If you know of any towns we should go to next—"

"Timberson has some funny stuff," Orville said. "So I hear."

It took all PJ's might to keep a straight face. "Thanks. We'll be sure to head up that way next."

Instead, he turned and walked back to Grant, who was watching the loud soldiers with mild interest. PJ sat next to him and sighed, wondering if he'd ever feel like he knew what he was doing.

"What do you think?" Grant asked.

"I think the dragon just wanted us to save Benny. I don't think there was more to it than that," PJ said with a defeated sigh. He still felt like he was missing something, but exactly what he didn't know. Maybe he was just overthinking it.

"Fair enough." Grant slapped him on the

shoulder. "You know, you aren't going to get this right the first few times."

"Yeah, I guess you're right. I—" PJ frowned, his gaze drawing to the center of the market square, where Quentin stood with a flock of bright, golden butterflies fluttering around him.

"That's odd," Grant said.

But he wasn't just standing there, and they weren't just fluttering.

They were *attacking* him.

Quentin flailed, kicked, and punched the air to no avail, crying out for someone to help him. He backed into one of the farmer's stands, falling onto it and shattering the wooden counter, sending produce flying. The butterflies continued their onslaught, diving at Quentin's face and clothes now that he was on his back.

"Somebody do something!" a woman screamed, snapping PJ out of his stupor.

He took a few steps toward the soldier, unsure what he could *actually* do, but as he drew closer, instinct (or the dragon) seemed to take over. He sensed the magic in the air, the *intention* behind the butterflies, and the thread that had originated somewhere to the east. He looked down at Quentin, inhaling deeply before opening his mouth wide and exhaling, the dragon's breath mingling with his own. There wasn't any fire, not even a hint of smoke, but the magic that flowed out of him was powerful enough to break whatever spell had been cast on these butterflies. They stopped, fluttering angrily for a moment, before taking off toward the blue sky above.

The dragon retreated to wherever it lived in PJ's mind, and he felt in control of his body once more. Quentin had curled into a ball, protecting his head as he whimpered, unaware that the butterflies had stopped attacking.

PJ knelt and reached out his hand. "You're okay. They're gone now."

Quentin flinched, looking around wildly, before his gaze landed on PJ. His face was covered in tiny scratches, and his clothes were torn in places—odd wounds from what should've been delicate insects. Someone had clearly wanted to hurt Quentin, though they had an interesting way of going about it.

"Quentin," PJ tried again when the soldier said nothing. "They're gone. You're safe now. Come on up. That's a good man."

The soldier scrambled to his feet, still breathing

heavily as he looked around. Behind PJ, a crowd had gathered, murmuring questions about what had happened. PJ wasn't sure himself, nor was he entirely sure how he'd made it *stop*, but before he could ponder that further, Grant's hand clamped down on his arm and pulled him away from the soldier.

"What in the world was *that*?" Grant whispered.

"Butterflies?" PJ replied, squinting at the sky. "Angry butterflies."

"No, not that. *You*." Grant let go of his arm. "How did you stop it?"

"I don't know," PJ said, grateful the dragon, at least, had known what to do. "I just sort of…" He swallowed, noticing the whispered conversations around them and not wanting to be overheard. "Let's talk about it later. I want to make sure Quentin's okay."

He left Grant and returned to the soldier, who was sitting on one of the overturned produce crates next to the stand he'd destroyed. Someone had brought him a wet rag, and someone else had found a blanket to put around his shoulders. But he'd regained his faculties, because when PJ approached, he jumped to his feet and pointed an accusatory finger at the teen.

"You!" he bellowed, causing everyone in the vicinity to turn their head toward PJ. "It was *you*!"

"I didn't—" PJ stammered as Grant came up beside him.

"You came to town to look for magical problems, so you made sure there was one," Quentin said, pointing between the two of them.

PJ turned to Grant, glaring daggers at him.

"Oh, come now," Grant said with a nervous laugh. "We told you we sensed a magical problem here! Now there is one. Why do you think we were hanging out in the town square? Because we knew we'd find our magical mischief here. And lo and behold, here it was."

The crowd murmured amongst themselves, and PJ was shocked that some of them actually believed what Grant was saying.

Quentin, on the other hand, seemed a hair smarter than that. "A likely story. Now, I suspect you'll want us to pay you a few gold coins to stop it, eh? Well, we're not going to fall for this trick. You charlatans can—"

"We aren't going to ask for any gold," PJ said, holding up his hands.

Grant cleared his throat, giving PJ a silencing look. "Look, me and my associate need to discuss what happened and get some witness statements. I'm sure we'll have this solved by dinnertime—"

"Let's not put a timeline on it," PJ muttered with an elbow to Grant's chest.

"Fine, fine. But rest assured, Firewing Investigations is *on* it!"

"What in the world is going on out here?" Mary pushed through the crowd, flanked by Abigail and another woman who was carrying a stack of papers. "You two. What have you done?"

"Saved a man's life," Grant said, before anyone else could say anything. "Quentin here seems to be the victim of a magical attack."

"Is that so?" Abigail said, glaring at them.

"We all saw it," the farmer whose stand had been destroyed said. "Outta nowhere. Big flock of golden butterflies. Scratched up his face and his clothes. Look at him!"

"And very *clearly*, we have a new element in town," a nearby queen's soldier said, looking at Grant and PJ. "I say it's them."

"They said they were in town to find magical mischief!"

"Quentin's right! They're the ones who caused it!"

"Make a problem just to cash in on solving it. I know this game!"

"Everyone calm down," Mary barked, looking around before settling her gaze on Grant and PJ. "Why don't you two *fine gentlemen* come to my office? We can talk about what you might or might not have done, and what your business is in town."

"They're magic hunters," Quentin said. "Or so they said."

"Really?" Abigail said, looking at PJ with a frown. "Why didn't you—"

"We weren't sure there was magic here," PJ said, his insides twisting as he lied to her. "But clearly, there is, so…"

"They said they were in Dag Flanigan's crew," Quentin continued, dabbing his cuts with a cloth soaked in alcohol. "Don't know if there's any way to verify that. Anyone could say anything. Especially two miscreants—"

"He was in Pigsend the same time you were, right, Abigail?" Grant said with a charming smile.

Abigail nodded, though she clearly didn't want to.

"Well, he stuck around after the solstice. We got to know him the second time he was in town, hunting a dragon shifter," Grant continued, flashing his teeth. "He took us under his wing. We didn't get *that* long with him, but enough to know where to sense when magic is about to make itself known. And, by golly, it looks like we've found it here."

Abigail's nostrils flared, but Mary spoke. "We'll sort all this out. Quentin, let us know if you need anything. Might be wise for you to head home and recuperate."

"I'm fine," he said, though his hands still were

shaking as he applied the salve to his wounds.

"Please, dear," Mary said with a kind smile. "You're no good to us like this. We'll be fine without you for a few hours."

He sniffed, but two farmers chimed in and prodded him, so he relented. But he didn't leave without giving PJ and Grant a parting sneer. "I still say it was that one. He did summin' funny to the butterflies to get 'em to leave. What's to say he didn't call 'em on me, too?"

"We'll be sure to talk with them about it," Mary said, turning to the boys. "You two. Come with me."

PJ and Grant were led to a large office with a placard that read *Mary Helmsberg, Mayor of Gilramore*, where they were left alone while Mary and Abigail convened just outside. PJ could only catch wisps of their conversation, but he had a feeling they probably weren't going to eat at the Wersts' dinner table this evening.

"Suppose the you-know-what was on to something," Grant whispered. "Have you ever seen anything like that before?"

PJ looked toward the door, still hearing the whispered conversations happening just beyond, and leaned closer to Grant. "Someone cast a spell to hurt Quentin."

"Obviously."

"I mean." PJ sighed. "I don't know how to explain it, but there was *intent* behind the magic. I've never felt anything like that before."

"How much magic have you been around?" Grant asked, glancing toward the closed door. "Maybe that's just how it feels."

PJ blew air between his lips. "Someone attacked him for a reason."

"So probably *not* a you-know-what?" Grant whispered.

"I can't rule it out completely," PJ said. "The grannies said there could be any kind of strange happenings, not just barns collapsing or things being set on fire. It's entirely possible someone's you-know-what magic is manifesting as butterflies. Maybe they just had a vendetta against Quentin and lost control of their power as they grow closer to their shift." He nodded toward the door. "Ergo, if we figure out who's got it in for him, we might find our you-know-what."

"But butterflies?" Grant made a face. "That doesn't seem like—"

"We need to turn over every stone," PJ said, recalling the grannies' letter.

"Yeah, but this stone happens to be in a town where people don't love anything to do with magic. I think it might be wise to let this one be and make our escape. I'm not sure they're going to let us stay after—"

"After you told them we were here to investigate magical problems moments before there was a magical problem?" PJ said with a look.

"I'm not the one who attacked a random guy with butterflies." Grant sniffed as he sat back. "And I mean, butterflies? Of all the things… I mean, who attacks with *butterflies*?"

"I don't know," PJ said. In fact, what he knew about magic, magical creatures, and anything to do with the concept couldn't fill the small bag he carried with him. In hindsight, it seemed rather odd that the grannies had dropped this task in his lap without as much as a book or discussion about what he might encounter, other than "there will be a lot of dead ends."

The dragon growled menacingly in the back of his mind, reminding PJ he was there. But, of course, he had nothing else to offer.

"Maybe there's another coin in it," PJ said, shifting to the one thing he knew could convince Grant to stick around. "Maybe a gold this time."

"I wish there was a way to know how much we'd get," Grant said. "Like five gold coins for every town saved, or—"

"Why, do you want to make sure it's worth your while?" PJ asked dryly. "If the dragon's only going to give you a silver, you're not going to bother?"

He shrugged.

"What would Bev do?" PJ said, looking at Grant.

"What?"

"What would Bev do if she were here?" He gestured to the office. "When earthquakes and sinkholes threatened the town of Pigsend, did she just say, 'Nope, that's too dangerous'?"

Grant snorted.

"When the Harvest Festival—"

"I get it," he said. "But we're not Bev. And nobody was threatening to run her out of town, either."

"What do you think would've happened had she not led the grannies to me?" PJ asked, lowering his voice and leaning over to whisper. "If Dag Flanigan had found me first?"

"I mean, Valta and I were the ones who—"

"Grant."

"*Fine.*" Grant let out a breath. "Fine. You're too noble. But you listen here." He poked the amulet underneath PJ's shirt. "We'd better be able to afford to sleep in inns after we find whoever did this, understand? I ain't sleeping in hay, or against a tree, or anything like that from here on out, got it?"

The amulet, predictably, didn't respond.

"Either way, the spell was coming from

somewhere east of here," PJ said. "So if we do manage to get out of here without being arrested, we should head in that direction."

"How'd you stop it anyway?" Grant glanced out the door to make sure the other two were still in conversation. "Your eyes got a little red."

"Dragon's breath," PJ said, his voice barely a whisper. "Don't ask me what that is or how it works or what it does. I just know it worked to break the spell." He chewed his lip. "I think our first question to the mayor and Abigail should be who might have it in for Quentin."

"I think a better question is who doesn't," Grant said. "He seems like the type to be in everyone's business. Maybe he stumbled on something he shouldn't have."

"In a town this size?" PJ asked.

"What? People still got secrets in small towns."

Mary and Abigail walked back into the office. Neither one looked happy as Mary sat in her chair and Abigail stood behind her with her arms crossed.

"Well, now, we do have a situation on our hands, don't we?" Mary said after a long pause. "Why don't you tell us what happened—starting with the *real* reason you've come to Gilramore?"

"We were walking by the river—" Grant started, but PJ cleared his throat.

"And ran into Byron fishing," he finished,

before Grant got the other man in trouble. "We struck up a conversation, mentioned Pigsend, and he invited us to dinner."

"Why were you even coming this way?" Abigail said.

"As we told you, we left Sheepsburg in search of our fortune," Grant said.

"Why did you need to sleep in my loft, then?"

"Because we're still searching for that fortune."

"And does that entail causing problems in perfectly fine towns with no magical mischief?" Mary asked. "Because to our eyes—"

"We didn't attack Quentin," PJ said.

"You did something to those butterflies," Mary said. "Three witnesses said you were able to disperse them."

"Because he was trained by Dag Flanigan on how to repel magic," Grant replied without missing a beat.

It really was quite incredible to watch him lie. It seemed to come as easily to him as breathing. Meanwhile, PJ had to dig his fingernails into his palm to keep a neutral face. He chafed at the idea that Flanigan had taught him anything other than terror.

Grant remained blissfully ignorant of PJ's discomfort. "That's kind of necessary in our line of work, you know?"

"And why didn't you mention that you worked for Mr. Flanigan last night at dinner?" Abigail said.

"It's not something we advertise, considering the current climate," Grant said with a shrug. "The wrong town, the wrong people. He got on lots of folks' bad sides. Best to keep information close to the vest." He gestured toward the door. "We got a tip that something magical was about to happen. That's why we were in the town square. We certainly didn't *cause* it."

"Someone wanted to hurt Quentin," PJ said. He couldn't lie nearly as well as Grant, so he decided to stay as close to the truth as possible. "It was clear when I got close enough to disperse the magic. Does he have any enemies?"

"Anyone who fought for the king," Mary said. "But we're getting off track. It's entirely possible he was just an easy target for your mischief. Are you here to extort us? Promise you'll make the attacks stop as long as we fork over a huge sack of gold?"

"No." PJ frowned. "That's not it at all. We're not expecting anything in return."

"Then how will you make your *fortune*?" Mary asked with a look.

"What my friend *means* to say is that we'll get payment *afterward*," Grant said, giving PJ a meaningful look. "Because it doesn't make sense to do all this work without expectation of some reward. *Obviously*, right, PJ?"

PJ caught his meaning—it might look more suspicious if they didn't ask for some sort of reward. "Y-yeah. But you can pay us whatever you think is fair. After we solve the problem, of course."

Mary and Abigail shared a long look, seemingly discussing the issue silently. Then Mary turned to them, sighing heavily as if she carried the weight of the world on her shoulders.

"Fine. You're hired." She cleared her throat. "But you should know that Quentin isn't the first victim."

PJ sat back, surprised. "Really?"

"So why'd you go through all that trouble asking if we're here to extort you if you knew we had nothing to do with it?" Grant said.

"As you said, we can't be too careful these days," Mary said. "There are lots of charlatans out to make quick coin. But it's clear you at least know how to *stop* the attacks as they're in progress, which is more than we had before."

PJ nodded, grateful they hadn't asked him to go into detail. "What happened the first time?"

"It was three days ago, long before you two showed up," Mary said. "Everything about that attack was the same as Quentin's. The victim was only able to escape by running into his home."

"How come no one else mentioned it?" Grant asked.

"The victim agreed to keep mum about the whole thing, especially because we thought..." She cleared her throat. "The first victim was a registrar. He perhaps made a few enemies as he went about his job. Some kingside soldiers didn't particularly like his methods of keeping up with them."

"I see," PJ said, recalling what the farmer had said about registrars taking advantage of their wards.

"We just assumed one of those soldiers had come for some revenge, now that the queen was gone," Mary said. "But Quentin wasn't a registrar. He was just a regular soldier."

"Got it," PJ said with a nod. "Could we go talk with this registrar? What was his name?"

"Burt Gibbons. But he's already left town," Mary said with a shake of her head. "Which is why I thought the problem had been dealt with. But clearly someone has a message they want to get across."

"Tell me everything you can about Quentin and this other registrar," PJ said.

In truth, not much that connected them, other than service to the queen, which could apply to everyone in town, save the farmers. Quentin had grown up in Gilramore; the registrar was from the other side of the country. They didn't even live on the same side of the town, with Burt next to the Wersts' property and Quentin north of town.

"I think the first thing we need to do is talk with Quentin again," PJ said, looking at Grant. "Find out if anyone's been threatening him." He turned back to the mayor and Abigail. "I know this town is pretty anti-magic. So there shouldn't be anyone magical around here, right?"

"That's correct." Mary shook her head firmly. "Absolutely nothing to speak of. And if there were, they're long gone. The queen's soldiers made sure of that."

"Well, we do have a mystery on our hands," Grant said, almost looking excited as he rose. "We'll be in touch." He nodded toward Abigail. "Still on for dinner tonight?"

She wrinkled her nose, as if she'd forgotten her promises to PJ already. "Erm, well…"

"We'll find our own way," PJ said, saving her from the embarrassment of turning them away. It was clear their new jobs hadn't made her trust them any more, and he could sense she wanted to keep them away from her children as much as possible. "We'll let you know what we find out."

~

"How are we gonna make our own way if we

don't have any coin, Peej?" Grant muttered, walking out of the town hall. "I'm not sleeping under a tree again."

"We'd better get to figuring out this butterfly problem, then," PJ retorted. "So what kind of creature attacks with butterflies?"

"You think I know?" Grant retorted. "You're the expert in this stuff. Ask the person in your head."

PJ hadn't heard much from the dragon, and it certainly hadn't provided any encyclopedic knowledge of magical creatures.

"He's not talking right now," PJ said, looking around. The crowd had thinned from the chaos earlier, though there were still people milling about, staring at the sky as if another flock of murderous winged insects would fly down and attack them at any moment. But he didn't spot the only victim still in town. "Where's Quentin?"

"The mayor did tell him to go home," Grant said. "Maybe he listened. Suppose we'll have to talk to him the next time he shows up to harangue us."

PJ gazed around the square, noticing the farmer whose stand had been destroyed—Orville. Quentin hadn't intentionally fallen into it, PJ assumed, but it had been destroyed all the same. Perhaps that farmer was in some way connected—and if not, he could shed some light on who might have it in for Quentin.

"You know, the grannies always rebuilt stuff when it was destroyed," PJ said, leisurely turning to Grant. "They said it was the right thing to do, but what if it was more than that?"

"Not following."

"I mean, the farmers knew a lot about the town before the queen's folks came," PJ said, nodding to Orville. "Maybe if we help him rebuild his stand, he'll tell us something he wouldn't have otherwise."

"Or we could just ask him what we want to ask him and avoid the rebuilding," Grant said, thumbing his nose. "You know I'm terrible with a hammer."

That was true. He'd lasted fifteen minutes with PJ's father in the farrier's shop back in Pigsend. "Fine." PJ straightened. "You go work on Quentin, then."

"Ugh. Do I have to?" Grant pouted.

"Yes." PJ gave him a meaningful glance. "If you want to sleep at the inn tonight, we have to earn our money."

"I don't even know where to look for him."

"I'm sure Mary or Abigail could steer you in the right direction," PJ said, walking toward the farmer. "I have all the faith in the world in you."

Grant grumbled but didn't disagree, stuffing his hands in his pockets and turning to walk back toward the town hall. PJ cautiously approached the destroyed farm stand, where Orville was muttering to himself as he gathered the fruit that had been scattered all over the ground. PJ bent down to pick up a few apples and walked them over with a smile. "I'm sorry about your stand."

"I'm sure you are, considering—"

"It wasn't me," PJ said.

The farmer eyed him for a moment.

"I did stop it, though," PJ said, thinking the farmer might've seen him do a bit more than the rest of the crowd from his vantage point. "Did you notice anything before the attack started?"

He shook his head, relaxing a bit as he inspected an apple and tossed it back into a nearby crate. "Nope. The usual nonsense from Quentin. Walking around like he owns the place. Then the butterflies came outta the sky, made a beeline for him, and you saw the rest."

"They came from the east, didn't they?" PJ said, hoping he sounded conversational.

Orville shrugged. "I didn't see them until they were attacking him."

PJ nodded, picking up another apple. "Do you have any supplies? Spare planks? Nails?"

The farmer surveyed him suspiciously. "Why?"

"We need to get your stand back together," PJ said, trying to act as if his offer were the most normal thing possible. The grannies had sort of barged their way into the wreckage and just started hammering back in Pigsend. Perhaps if PJ just got to work, the farmer might not question too much more.

"Well, erm… I do have some planks back at my barn," Orville said, rubbing the back of his neck. "It's a bit of a walk, but—"

"I'm happy to go with you." PJ smiled and hoped it looked friendly. "Let's get going so you aren't out a farm stand too much longer."

Although he seemed leery, Orville agreed to take PJ back to his home to get the supplies. Which meant they were off to a good start, as long as Grant was doing *his* job and talking with Quentin. He was vastly more charming than PJ and could get people to talk when they didn't want to.

PJ, on the other hand, was still terrible at lying, so he hoped he'd earn the farmer's trust by telling him about who he was and where he'd come from. That, at least, he didn't have to lie too much about.

"Farrier, eh?" Orville said, as PJ told him about his childhood in Pigsend. "How'd you get in with the queen's people?"

PJ parroted the same story Grant had told Abigail and Mary and found that his words came a little easier when he already had a story to stick to.

The farmer nodded, though he didn't seem quite as impressed as the others had been. "So you think someone attacked Quentin? Who could it be?"

"I was hoping you could help me figure that out," PJ said. "Right now, I'm thinking it's someone who had a vendetta against the queen. Know anyone who might fit that description?"

Orville laughed. "I'm a simple farmer. I stay out of queen and king and back-to-queen and back-to-king stuff. I just pick my apples, tend to my farm animals, and keep my head down."

"Probably wise," PJ said. "Has anything like this ever happened in Gilramore before?" Mary had said she'd kept the first attack quiet, but gossip tended to have a way of working itself out in towns like this.

"Never seen anything like it in these parts. Even before the queen invaded. People had magic, of course, but nobody ever used it like *that*. We've always been pretty peaceful."

"You've lived here a long time?"

Orville nodded. "My whole life."

"Was it always…" PJ thumbed toward the town that had disappeared in the rolling hills. "So loyal to the queen?"

"Nah. We were just a small farming village. Wasn't but two or three shops in the main square, and those were mostly for farming supplies. We didn't even have an inn."

"I wonder why the queen chose this place for

her registrars?"

"You have the Wersts to thank for that," he said. "I don't know the whole story, but Byron brought his new bride back from somewhere, and before we knew it, the town was transformed. They built the inn, the registrars' offices, the town hall, all those new shops—blacksmith, tannery, uniform shop, all the rest." He snorted. "Didn't bother us farmers much. Used to have to take our wares up the road an hour to Timberson to sell 'em. Now we can just walk into town. And I planted a whole new grove to keep up with demand."

PJ nodded. "What's happened now that the queen's been defeated?"

"Not much—at least, not yet. Everyone's in a bit of shock. I think it took our mayor a few weeks to even accept that the letter she'd gotten wasn't a practical joke. But then we started getting the magical folks passing through, and, well, that sort of sealed the deal for us. Some of the registrars decided to leave, others have stuck around, though there's nothing for them to do lately." He eyed PJ. "Awfully convenient you and your friend were here when this strange magic occurred."

"We've got a sense for things," PJ said. "Comes with our previous experience." He really did need to get better at lying if he was going to stick with Grant. "We had a hunch something magical was going to happen, but we didn't know what."

"How can you have a hunch something magical's about to happen?"

PJ sighed, realizing he might have to give up one secret to gain this farmer's trust. "Well, to be honest, it wasn't so much a hunch as good luck. We were passing by when I heard Benny Werst being swept down the creek."

Orville gasped and looked at him. "No!"

"He's fine," PJ said, holding up his hands. "I jumped in and pulled him out. Got to talking with his father, who invited us to stay for a meal and a night."

Orville's brows furrowed. "The creek was high yesterday. What in the world was he doing swimming—"

"Fishing with his father. He fell in." PJ gave Orville a knowing smile as he tapped his nose. "We're not telling Abigail."

"Ah." He nodded. "She does tend to rule the roost over there."

"In any case, Grant and I were trying to decide whether to stick around or keep moving when Quentin was attacked." PJ looked up at the sky. "Magic hunting isn't an exact science, unfortunately. But we got lucky this time." A bird flew overhead, cawing as he went.

The farmer gave him a sideways glance. "How

long have you been doing this *investigating* anyway?"

"Not too long on our own," PJ said, grateful he could be truthful about that, in any case. "Mayor Helmsberg hired us to look into it. Fees to be discussed after the work is done, of course," he added quickly, as Orville gave him another suspicious look. "We're not grifters. Just two young men looking to help a world turned upside down."

Orville didn't look impressed. "Well, come on. It's right up here."

PJ should've probably recognized from the apples he'd picked up in the square that Orville owned the apple trees by the river—the ones Grant had stolen from when they'd saved Benny. PJ was happy he could repay the farmer by helping him with his stand. Two apples didn't seem worth that much, but it was still theft.

"I've got the wood right here," Orville said, walking him over to a pile of freshly milled planks. "Nails are in the barn."

"Right-o."

PJ found a bag of nails and a hammer, being careful to hold the hammer by the wooden hilt. Which made him realize that rebuilding this stand might be a *tad* harder than anticipated. Magic and iron didn't mix, so he'd have to hide the way the iron zapped him, as it had when he'd tried to help his father shoe horses with wholly iron tools after he'd come into his powers.

How did the grannies handle it?

Perhaps they just got used to the feeling. PJ would have to toughen up, he supposed.

They returned to the square, where the crowd hadn't yet dissipated. PJ scanned their faces for Quentin and didn't see him—nor did he see Grant. Abigail and Mary stood in front of the destroyed farm stand, and both seemed surprised to find PJ returning with Orville, supplies in hand.

"What are you doing?" Abigail asked.

"Helping," PJ said, carefully laying the planks on the ground. "Anything else happen while I was gone?"

"N-no," Mary said, watching as he picked up the long string of tanned leather to measure the broken counter piece and laid it against the new piece of wood. "You're really rebuilding this stand?"

"Why wouldn't I?" PJ said, marking where he needed to cut and picking up the saw.

He wasn't skilled in carpentry, but he could cut wood and hammer nails. And, he mused, the longer he searched the country for shifters, the better he'd get at it. No wonder the grannies were able to rebuild anything.

Abigail and Mary took Orville aside, presumably to ask him what he and PJ had talked about, and PJ kept working, humming to himself as he did. He reached into the bag of iron nails and braced himself for the sting of pain, but while there was a small shock, it was quite muted. He pulled one nail out and held it between his fingers. The pain was on par with a small mosquito bite.

"Interesting," PJ muttered to himself.

He became aware that Abigail was watching him, so he busied himself with actually hammering the nail into the wood. He did discover that putting the nails between his teeth earned him more of a shock but was able to hide his reaction.

Still the question of *why* the iron wasn't hurting him as much as it had been stuck in his mind. The only thing that had changed between Pigsend and now was his new amulet. But it had made him more sensitive to magic, so the iron should hurt worse, right? Or was the magic in his bones so powerful that it overpowered iron? Was that even a thing?

More questions for the grannies.

The longer he spent on this quest, the more he worried he was in over his head. The dragon had been quiet since the butterflies, and it certainly wasn't chatty when it did speak to him.

He finished hammering another nail and looked at the sky. Perhaps he'd send a letter once they figured out what was happening. Gilramore was too anti-magic for him to feel comfortable writing unless he absolutely needed to. Especially with the way Abigail was glaring at him.

"Trust your instincts," he muttered to himself. "They haven't steered you wrong before."

CHAPTER SEVEN

The farm stand wasn't that big, so by the time Mary and Abigail had finished interrogating Orville, PJ had the frame already reconstructed and was measuring the planks for the front apron.

"You're not half bad, you know," Orville said, walking over. "Thank you for your help."

"That's why I'm here," PJ said, as he put the first plank on and hammered in two nails. "What did the mayor want to talk with you about?"

"You, of course." Orville chuckled as he handed PJ another plank, then started measuring another to cut. "They're wondering what you're up to."

"What'd you tell them?" PJ asked.

"Well, I told them I thought you were an

industrious young man who seems eager to make your mark on the world," he said. "Seems like you came at just the right time, too." He cleared his throat. "Didn't mention to Ms. Werst about her son falling in the river. Byron's a friend—he cut this wood into planks for me a few days ago—so I think he'd be mad with me if I spilled his secrets."

PJ chuckled. "They have a nice family."

"Yeah, the boys are a hoot. And little Margo is certainly eager to keep up with them." He picked up the saw to cut the plank. "Anyway, I tried to tell 'em they should let you do your job, but…"

PJ followed his gaze and found the mayor and head registrar watching him with suspicion. "I can't say I blame them. I told them I was going to investigate a magical mishap, but I'm over here rebuilding a stand. Probably looks like I'm not doing what I'm supposed to be doing."

"You're helping the town." He handed PJ the cut plank and started measuring another. "Can't say I find fault with that."

PJ nodded, putting the wood in place and considering his next question carefully. "So these registrars. I heard some of them weren't so nice."

"Yeah." He chuckled. "I mean, I don't know specifics, of course, but a lot of 'em skipped town as soon as they found out the king was back on the throne."

"I heard about one of them," PJ said. "Burt something?"

"Gibbons. He was pretty rude, but not quite as bad as…" Orville shivered. "Well, if you haven't met Carl, you will soon. He's the one who's too loud and too rude and hangs around the square."

PJ nodded. "And Quentin, too? Does he run in that circle?"

Orville laughed. "Nah. Quentin acts tough, but he wilts like a flower when it comes to putting those bullies in line." He rubbed his chin. "But I will tell ya that amongst the locals there *was* a lot of…well, not-so-nice feelings toward Quentin when he first joined the queen's army."

"In what way?" PJ asked. "I thought the town was loyal to the queen?"

"Nah, we didn't care one way or another. It's all the new folks who came to town. And the handful of locals who threw their lot in with the queen. 'Course, I think Quentin's was just self-preservation. Better to join 'em than end up in prison."

"Why would he go to prison?" PJ asked.

"Well, 'cause he has magic," Orville said.

PJ almost hit his thumb with the hammer. "*What?*"

"Not a whole lot, not enough for the queen to consider dangerous," he said. "Else he would've been carted off with the rest of 'em."

"Who else was arrested by the queen?" PJ asked. "I thought there weren't any other magical folks around?"

"There was a family of witches who lived a ways east of town." He shook his head. "All of 'em got carted away, to my knowledge. I..." He shifted uncomfortably. "Now I don't know this for sure, but I hear Quentin might've been the one to sell 'em out. Maybe as a show of loyalty to the queen, you know?"

Certainly a motive. "I sent my associate Grant to talk with him. Maybe he's found out something."

"Doubtful. Quentin's always acted like he's more important than anyone else, and for him to be so publicly humiliated..." He chuckled. "If you want to learn something about Gilramore, you're going to want to head to the inn tonight. Most everyone in town likes to eat there, even the farmers. Ygritte—she's the farmer with a stand right next to mine—she's there every night, practically. You'll probably hear more than you want to. This town loves gossip."

"As all small towns do." PJ finished hammering the last of the boards then ran his hand along the front, making sure he hadn't missed anything. "Well, that should do it, I think."

"Good as new," Orville said.

"Do you need help getting all your tools back

home?" PJ asked.

"No, no. You've done plenty." He beamed and held out his hand. "Thank you so much for your help. Really glad you came to town, whatever brought you here."

"My pleasure—"

Something *thumped* on the ground nearby.

Orville stooped to pick it up. "Oh, you must've dropped this, eh?"

He turned over his hand, revealing a gold coin. PJ stared at it for a moment then took it gratefully from the farmer. "I suppose I must have. T-thank you." He swallowed, gathering his bearings again, and beamed. "Let me know if there's anything else I can do for you."

Because very clearly, he would be paid handsomely for it.

~

PJ pocketed the gold and bade Orville farewell, eager to find Grant and discuss what he'd learned. He hoped his friend hadn't shirked his responsibilities, but PJ also wasn't holding his breath. Grant had a great many good qualities, but when the going got tough... Well, there was a reason they'd dropped out of university. Still, now they had a gold coin, which could hopefully pay for a meal and a room at the Gilramore Inn that evening. A good start.

He did a loop around the small town in search of Grant, and as he walked, he turned over the few threads he'd gathered in his mind. The family of witches had been an interesting discovery, as was the fact that Quentin had sold them out (if Orville was to be believed). It was odd Mary hadn't mentioned them, though she'd said anyone with magic was long gone. But as they'd learned back in Sheepsburg, people who were supposedly "long gone" were returning. Was it possible the witch family had come back and wanted revenge? Or was there something else afoot he didn't know about? His task was definitely made more difficult as he was just starting to scratch the surface of the town's people and personalities. But at least he'd made one friend, and Orville had definitely given him more than he'd had before.

It seemed, then, that his instinct to help first and ask questions later was the right one. The grannies had certainly been at the scene of every shop fire and barn destruction, rebuilding with cheery smiles and not a whiff of what they were really doing. He had no clue if they'd faced the same distrust and uncertainty from the towns they went to. If they'd met such a reaction in Pigsend, they'd never mentioned it.

Although PJ had cleared his mind, the walk proved otherwise fruitless, as Grant was nowhere to be found. But as he returned to the square to ask around, he spotted Quentin marching back to his position near Orville's farm stand. His uniform appeared a size too small, and he'd applied cloth bandages over the worst of his injuries. On the whole, he didn't look too roughed up, except he kept glancing toward the sky to make sure he wasn't about to be attacked again.

"How are you?" PJ asked, walking up to him.

"Fine, no thanks to you," Quentin said, not meeting his gaze. "They're saying you did it—"

"Who's they?" PJ asked.

Quentin shifted. "People."

So, no one. "Did my associate Grant talk with you?"

"No."

"Did he try?" PJ asked.

"Don't care."

PJ swallowed the instinct to snap back at him. "We're trying to find the person who did this to you. Surely, that merits a little friendlier conversation."

"Why do you care?" Quentin asked. "You're a stranger. Passing through. I'm sure you're just out to extort me. Well, I don't have any coin—"

PJ blew air between his lips. Surely, the grannies encountered this kind of resistance, too. How did they handle it?

With unflappable kindness, he told himself. *Same as Bev.*

"I'm not looking to be paid, but I do want to help," PJ said, pointing to Orville. "I got Orville's stand back up and running."

"Wasn't my fault his stand was in the way."

PJ cleared his throat. "He and I got to talking. He mentioned something about witches."

Quentin shifted. "Don't know anything about witches."

"Orville mentioned you were…" PJ considered his words, and Quentin's lack of enthusiasm. "He mentioned you maybe had something to do with them being arrested a few years ago."

The soldier finally turned to him, fire in his gaze. "That farmer needs to keep his mouth shut. I did *nothing*. And if anyone says I did, they're *lying*." He pointed his finger at PJ and iron bangles popped up from under his too-short sleeves.

"What are those?"

"What do they look like?" He quickly covered them up, but they slid right back out. The skin underneath was pinkish and calloused.

PJ could only imagine how painful wearing iron all day, every day might get for someone with magic. "Don't they hurt?"

"Not too bad. I ain't got that much magic to begin with. My *father* took all that with him—along with everything else."

The way he said *father* told PJ there was quite a story there, and he wasn't sure it had anything to do with Quentin's father's magic. But there was something in his voice that gave PJ pause. "Are you worried something will happen if you take them off?"

"No."

"Then why—"

"Because I don't want anyone getting any ideas about my loyalties," he said gruffly. "I threw my lot in with the queen." He paused, perhaps reassessing his words. "I mean, I was happy to do it, of course. Nobody threatened me or anything. Just the best course of action. Magical people should be kept away from the rest of the normal folks." He sniffed. "Folks like *my father* who went from town to town, promising the moon and leaving nothing but a burden behind."

"Ah." PJ nodded in understanding. "I see."

"Course, he got what he deserved. I told the queen's folks *just* where to find him." He smirked. "That was right after I—"

"Told them about the witch family?" PJ asked.

Quentin started, color rising to his pale cheeks. "Yeah, I told the queen's soldiers about 'em. If I hadn't, they would've taken *me*. I swore to 'em I'd be loyal—the iron bangles, you know. But they wanted more *proof,* so…" Sadness filled his eyes. "So that happened. Wasn't proud of it. But when all the new folks showed up in town, they were proud of me. Abigail Werst even gave me a medal for my bravery."

"She did, did she?" PJ rubbed his chin.

"She promised she'd look after me, too. Got me a spot in the queen's service locally after a while. Signed whenever I needed a signature." He puffed out his chest. "Really grateful to her husband for bringing her here. She's always looked out for me, and I have a soft spot for her two little boys."

PJ briefly debated telling him about Benny's swim the day before but decided against it. "Is it possible the witches have come back?"

"They were arrested—"

"People who were supposedly dead are showing up all over the place," PJ said. "They've all been in hiding, I suppose."

His gaze shot to the sky, expectantly. "N-no, I can't say I've seen them." He shook himself. "But wouldn't expect to, either. They're long gone."

"Then can you think of anyone who might want to attack you?" PJ asked.

"Well, I can think of *two* people who might want to earn some quick coin," Quentin said, eyeing PJ. "I felt whatever you did to those butterflies. I don't believe you're part of Dag Flanigan's crew.

Don't think he'd take on a kid who can break curses like that."

"You'd be surprised," PJ said. "Sometimes you gotta fight fire with fire."

"Hmph. Well. As a thank you for saving me, I won't tell anyone what I saw, what with your red eyes and loud rumbling noises."

"If you can think of anything else," PJ said, as he wasn't going to get more answers out of this soldier today, "please let me know. I really do want to help you, Quentin."

The soldier just tightened his jaw and said nothing.

~

PJ left Quentin at his post. He didn't see Grant anywhere, and he was growing a *bit* annoyed his friend had blown off the one thing PJ had asked him to do. Grant didn't have coin to be at the inn, so the one place he might be was—

"PJ!"

He spun, searching for the source of the small voice, and smiled when the two Werst boys came bounding up, their eyes wide and sparkling with excitement.

"Did you figure out what's happening?" Benny asked, almost breathlessly.

"Not yet," PJ said. "But I'm heading to your house, if you'd like to walk with me."

The boys readily agreed, and PJ couldn't help but laugh at their enthusiasm. They peppered him with all manner of questions about where he came from, and what he thought of this and that, and if he'd read this book their father had read to them last week.

"Can't say I have," PJ said as they left the town proper and walked the dirt road toward the Wersts' house.

"I'm sure you've been busy trying to find the evildoer in town," Benny said. "We're so lucky you showed up when you did. You're close to solving it, right?"

"I have some theories," he said with a shrug. "You two don't know anything about those witches who live out east, do you?"

"Only that Mom says they're gone, and they won't hurt us," Benny said. "Pascal used to have nightmares about them, but she told us that the queen's soldiers came by and made sure they were taken care of." He paused, looking up at PJ with a worried expression. "They aren't back, are they?"

PJ was torn between telling them the truth and easing their fears and decided on the latter. "I don't think so. But if you two have anything to tell me about the attacks—"

"Benny saw them—" Pascal started, but his brother elbowed him.

"You saw them?" PJ asked the other boy, narrowing his gaze."You weren't in the town square when Quentin was attacked, were you?"

Benny's cheeks reddened. "N-no, but at our neighbor's house. Mr. Gibbons. I saw the butterflies swoop down and attack him while he was planting flowers. He fought them off by running inside, but the flowers are still there. I haven't seen him in a few days, and Mom said he was taking a holiday to rest his weary bones."

"Can you show me?"

CHAPTER EIGHT

The boys led PJ toward a cottage on the other side of the small fence that surrounded their property. PJ kept his eyes and ears (both human and dragon) out for anything unusual, but as they walked down the path, he sensed nothing but a nice fall day. The kids chattered away about a story their father had told them the night before, and about the cookies Byron was going to make soon with the chocolate he'd gotten from a recent day trip to another town. PJ only half-listened, enough so the boys would think he was paying attention, but his mind was elsewhere, thinking about Quentin and what else he might be hiding.

"What do you two boys know about Quentin?" PJ asked.

"Only that our mom says we need to respect him, even though he's silly," Benny said.

PJ couldn't help the smile. "Silly?"

"He's weird. Always wearing that uniform and acting like he's in charge. Likes to tell us what to do, even though we never listen. Like he's the mayor or something."

"I saw him run away from mean people," Pascal added. "They called him names and said he wasn't a real member of the queen's service."

PJ hazarded a guess that was the aforementioned Carl. He'd find out more this evening. "Do you know why he wears those iron bangles?" PJ asked.

"Mom says it's because he likes them," Benny said.

"Perhaps he does," PJ murmured. "Did Mr. Gibbons wear the same iron bangles, too?"

They shook their heads

Worth a shot.

Burt Gibbons's cottage was uninhabited but locked. Besides the few extra leaves on the front porch, there didn't seem much amiss. PJ peeked inside the windows, looking for anything out of place.

"What can you tell me about your neighbor?" PJ asked.

"Well, he was..." Benny looked at Pascal. "He was mean. Never liked us to play in his yard. That's why Dad built that fence. We got chased off too many times."

"I see," PJ said, grateful the man was gone now. "Anything else? He was a big queen supporter, wasn't he?"

The boys stared at him, bewildered.

"Erm, never mind," PJ said. He wondered if they knew a world where someone *wasn't* a queen's supporter. They'd find out soon enough, he supposed. "Anything else?"

"Mommy helped him when the butterflies attacked him," Pascal said. "He came to talk to her, and she told him to leave town. I wasn't supposed to hear, but I did."

"Where did the attack happen?" PJ asked.

"Right here," Benny said, taking them around to the backyard. From the looks of it, Burt Gibbons had been in the middle of planting flowers, as there was a large, open hole by his back porch and a pile of unplanted flowers, roots and all, right next to it. Three or four of the flowers had already been planted, but the rest had been left to the elements.

"Hm." PJ knelt and picked up one of the flowers, sniffing the wilting, yellow bud. There was nothing interesting or magical about it—just a flower that hadn't been planted yet. He picked up the trowel that had been left on the ground and pushed some of the dirt out of the way, sticking the roots into the soil and covering the stem. Then he gazed at the sky, hoping he might see the flock of butterflies.

"What are you doing?" Benny asked.

"Helping," PJ said, grabbing the next flower. "Poor Mr. Gibbons will have to come home to dead flowers, and no one wants that. It's not that much trouble to plant them for him. And it might make him happy when he gets back."

He kept planting, stopping every so often to glance at the sky but finding nothing but puffy white clouds. The boys stepped in to help, eager to get their hands dirty, and PJ let them plant the last few while he searched for signs of attack. It didn't *seem* like planting the flowers was the trigger—but it had been a long shot, anyway. Quentin certainly hadn't been doing anything but standing there when he'd been attacked.

"I *know* you boys aren't getting filthy in Mr. Gibbons's yard." Abigail stood at the fence between her house and Mr. Gibbons's, hands resting on her hips.

PJ waved bashfully. "Sorry, Abigail, I saw these flowers and—"

"You two," Abigail said, thumbing back toward her house. "Get cleaned up. There are chores to do before dinner, and I'd better not see a speck of dirt being tracked inside."

Pascal said a hasty goodbye to PJ and hurried to get home, but Benny remained for a heartbeat longer.

"You're staying for dinner, right?" Benny asked, looking at PJ with wide eyes.

"PJ has lots of work to do," Abigail replied before PJ could. "Don't you?"

"Yeah, but we'll be around," PJ said, ruffling Benny's short hair. "If you see anything else, let me know, will you?"

"I sure will!"

The boy scampered after his brother, but PJ wisely remained where he was, sensing that Abigail was about to let him have it—and it had nothing to do with getting her two little boys dirty.

"What's your real story?" she asked, her voice low and menacing.

"I'm sorry?" PJ frowned. "I've told you—"

"Why did you help Orville rebuild his farm stand?" It sounded like an accusation. "And why didn't you ask him for money?"

"I was just trying to help," PJ said, as it was the closest thing to the truth he could offer.

"I don't trust you," Abigail said. "I don't like that you still haven't told me why you're really here, and I don't like that you're being so helpful." As she spoke, even she seemed to realize how ridiculous she sounded. "I don't want you anywhere near my boys, understand?"

"I don't mean them any harm," PJ said, holding up his hands.

"You had them trespassing on my neighbor's property," Abigail said.

"I mean, it's your neighbor," PJ said with a dubious look. "And it's also the site of the first attack. I just wanted to see—"

"There's nothing to see. It's much the same as the Quentin attack. I don't see how dragging my children onto his land will help you."

PJ clicked his tongue. "He supported the queen, yeah?"

Abigail nodded. "Everyone in town does. You'd be hard-pressed to find someone who didn't wholeheartedly love her."

Clearly, the farmers in the square hadn't shared their opinions with her. "Great. Just trying to turn every stone." He cleared his throat. "I'm actually off to find Grant so we can compare what we've found out today. Have you seen him?"

"You'll find him asleep in my hayloft," Abigail said with a sneer. "He's not quite as *helpful* as you are, it seems."

PJ had to bite the inside of his cheek to keep from scowling. "Well, I've still got more questions I need to ask the townsfolk, so—"

Her nostrils flared. "I can tell you whatever you need to know."

"Fine." PJ crossed his arms. "What do you know about the family of witches who lived east of here? And is there any chance they've returned?"

Her eyes widened, and she licked her lips as her gaze darted around. "Have you seen them?"

"Well, no, not that I know of," PJ said. "That's why I'm asking about them."

"They're gone. Were cleared out before we even started building in town," Abigail said with a firm nod. "And if that's your *only* idea, I don't think it's necessary for you to stick around. We can investigate ourselves. Goodness knows, Byron doesn't have enough to keep him busy—"

"Then why did Mayor Helmsberg ask us to stay?"

"She's desperate to solve the problem before things get out of hand," Abigail said, brushing off his concern with an impatient sigh. "But I'm sure there aren't going to be any more attacks. It was just a fluke. A random weather pattern. A group of insects who got caught in a windstorm and—"

"And viciously attacked a soldier?" PJ asked doubtfully. "After attacking another soldier days earlier?"

She waved him off, exasperated. "It just isn't

worth your time. If you're truly *trained by Dag Flanigan*, I'm sure you have more pressing matters to attend to in larger towns."

"Again, your mayor *asked* us to investigate," PJ said. "I'd say that warrants us hanging around at least another day or two."

"And are you planning on sleeping in my barn again?" She lifted her chin, almost daring him to argue with her. "Because if you *have* the coin to pay for the inn, but didn't, that raises questions in my mind about what kind of magic hunters you truly are."

"Your husband invited us to stay yesterday," PJ said, evenly. "You'll have to ask him the details."

Her nostrils flared.

"In fact," PJ continued, wanting to poke the bear just a little more. "We weren't planning to stay at all. We were just passing through when I got a strange sense about Benny."

"My Benny?" Abigail took a step back, horrified. "You must be mistaken. My children are completely normal."

"Then why are you so eager for us to be on our way?" PJ asked. "It seems to me you're hiding something."

The color rose on her cheeks, confirming PJ, at least, wasn't completely wrong. "My family is loyal to the queen. We had no magic or anything that would possibly garner *your* attention. And to say otherwise is…well, frankly, offensive. We've all been tested *extensively*, and we had nothing to do with Quentin's attack—if one could even call it that. It seemed like he was just overwhelmed by butterflies."

"Then why did you encourage Burt Gibbons to leave town?" PJ asked.

"You're barking up the wrong tree," Abigail said firmly. "Now, if you *don't* mind, please retrieve your *friend* and get off our property before I—"

PJ held up his hands. "That's exactly what I was on my way to do." He nodded. "Good day, Abigail. I'll see you around."

~

"Oh, are you back?" Grant said as PJ climbed up the ladder to the Wersts' barn. He looked quite cozy, nestled into the hay with his shirt over his head, and from the sleepiness in his gaze, he appeared to have been doing exactly what PJ had hoped he hadn't been.

"Did you have a good rest?" PJ asked, deciding against mentioning he'd earned a shiny new gold coin. "While I did all the work?"

"In case you forgot, I'm the one who got us hired." Grant laid back down and rested his hands behind his head. "After all that smart braining, I needed to rest. Can't keep a roof over our head if I can't think straight, you know."

PJ decided not to mention they'd just lost that roof. "Well, while you rested your poor, tired brain, I was busy learning what I could about the town and Quentin," he said. "And fixing Orville's stand."

"Who's Orville?"

PJ gave him a look.

"Right, the one who… Yeah." Grant cleared his throat. "So what's the story?"

"Did you even talk with Quentin?" PJ asked.

"I tried," Grant said. "He wouldn't open the door for me. And I'm not about to harass someone who's just been attacked. Poor form, you know."

"Well, if you'd waited in the town square, you might've learned something from him," PJ said, impatiently. "Because I had a chat with him."

"And?"

PJ told Grant everything he'd learned, including how Quentin might've earned some enemies amongst the magical sort in town—if they were still around—and how he still wore those iron bangles, even though the queen no longer mandated them.

"I think we should ask around about the family of witches. Wouldn't be a stretch to think if some of them had survived, they might be out for revenge. How they fit in with the other victim, I don't know."

"You think the witches attacked with butterflies?" Grant said. "Don't they have, I don't know, regular-looking magic? Besides that, I thought we were looking for dragons, not witches?"

PJ felt the weight of the amulet sitting around his neck. "We are. I'm just following a thread. Which is what we're supposed to do, instead of disappearing to sleep in barns we aren't supposed to be in."

"I spoke to a few folks, *thank you very much*," Grant said. "Nobody really wanted to chat, though. They all thought we did it." He snorted. "Maybe whoever did it will attack Quentin again. That'll loosen his tongue."

PJ looked out the door to the Wersts' house. "Abigail stopped me on the way here. She wants us out of her barn."

"No surprise there."

"And she's hiding something." PJ rose and went to the barn door, looking out at the house, where he assumed Abigail was standing, waiting at the window for them to leave. "She was adamant there was nothing to find in Gilramore. Which, of course, makes me all the more suspicious, considering there are butterflies attacking people. Do you think Mary's been hiding more attacks than Mr. Gibbons?"

"I say we let 'em have it. They want to solve their own problems, let's just get a move on. There's probably another town down the road being plagued by magical frogs that might want our help —and would pay for it."

"Not yet," PJ said. "Orville said a good chunk of the town eats at Gilramore Inn. Let's go there tonight, get some food, see what we can learn."

"With what money?" Grant said. "You were *just* getting on my case about—"

PJ pulled out the gold coin he'd earned earlier, and Grant's mouth fell open.

"Where'd you…" He nodded. "Fixing that old man's stand, eh?"

"See what happens when you're helpful?" PJ said, putting it back in his pocket. "I bet we'll get four times that if we find out who attacked Quentin and the others. Something to consider next time someone's property gets destroyed."

"And aren't we lucky you're so good with tools."

PJ snorted then paused, looking at his hands. "I was actually able to handle nails today."

"So?"

"So that's one thing I know," PJ said. "Iron and magic don't mix."

"Maybe you just have so much of it that it doesn't affect you anymore," Grant said. "I mean, you never used to have any issues before you wore that amulet."

"Yeah, but I hadn't become a dragon yet—"

"You've *always* been a dragon," Grant said. "The

only thing that changed was you could shift. I mean, with this new amulet, you've got more access to the dragon's senses. Maybe that means you're more powerful than iron, too"

PJ sat back, pulling the amulet out from under his shirt to inspect it. He'd certainly felt different when he'd put it on, and he'd never heard the dragon before. Never been *controlled* by him, either, like he'd been when the butterflies were attacking Quentin.

"Well, suppose we'd better get a move on if we want to make it to the inn for dinner," Grant said, stretching. "As I'm sure Ms. Werst is ready for us to make our exit from her property. Besides that…" He cracked a wry smile. "Sounds like we've got much nicer accommodations waiting for us there."

Grant had practically skipped out of the barn, insisting on carrying the gold coin and even checking it three times to make sure it was valid legal tender.

"I wonder how much gold is in the amulet. And where it comes from," he said, twirling the coin in his hand again. "Do you think it disappears after a while? Like it's fake money?"

"I don't think so," PJ said. "The grannies' money never disappeared."

"Then where does it come from?"

"Don't dragons have hoards?" PJ asked. "Maybe there's a huge pile of it somewhere buried beneath a mountain, and the amulet just summons it whenever it's needed."

"It's awfully stingy," Grant said. "I mean, you'd think it would just give us a chunk, you know?"

"I think it wisely senses you'd spend it all," PJ said. "So a coin here and there is how it's going to be."

The Gilramore Inn was right in the center of town, and as PJ walked inside, the scent of freshly-cut wood filled his nostrils. There were still homages to the queen hanging on the walls, from a tapestry depicting her face to her symbols and colors, and even a flag draped along the back wall. It was clear no one aligned against the queen would be welcome here. The innkeeper glared at them as if she knew they were up to no good. PJ recognized her as one of the crowd who'd gathered after Quentin had been attacked—and one of several who'd named them the culprits.

Grant, who was much better at charm than PJ, slid the gold coin over to the innkeeper. "One room, two beds, please. And dinner, of course." He looked around as if appraising the place. "It's such a lovely establishment."

The gold remained on the counter. "I don't let rooms to troublemakers," she said. "Nor do I serve 'em dinner."

Grant flashed her a charming smile. "Well,

aren't we so lucky that we aren't troublemakers. We just need one night. After all, we've been hired by your mayor to investigate the horrific attack on Quentin, and we do plan to get to the truth quickly."

"I heard she said *if* you figured out what happened, you might earn a small fee," the innkeeper said, clearly believing her mayor over Grant. "You know, I usually test people for magic before they stay here."

"C'mon." Grant flashed her a charming smile. "We've been *hired*. You can't expect us to sleep outside, can you? How are we supposed to find Quentin's attacker that way?"

PJ watched the innkeeper consider this, but after a long, *long* pause, she slid over a key with a clearly marked *four* on it. "Tick-tock. We ain't waiting around forever."

"My associate and I are working on it, I promise," Grant said with a loud chuckle. "But if you'd like to help, can you make sure we're seated next to someone who might—"

She rolled her eyes and disappeared back into the kitchen.

Grant made a face before turning to PJ. "Well, at least we have a place to sleep, eh?"

"I think the *best* idea is for us to keep our heads down tonight," PJ said. "We'll probably learn more by listening than dominating the conversation."

"You listen," Grant said, adjusting his shirt. "I've got my own talents. We'll see who comes up with more information by the end of the night." He cracked a smile, jamming the key into the door of their room. "Winner gets—"

"What?" PJ snorted as he brushed past Grant. "You have nothing to wager."

"Fine. Loser gets to rebuild the next thing that goes down," Grant said.

"I thought you didn't know how to swing a hammer?"

"I don't." He chuckled. "Which is why I'm going to win." He stretched and headed toward the stairs. "C'mon. There's a pair of comfortable beds with our name on them and several hours before dinner."

PJ couldn't deny it was nice to sleep on a mattress again. He stretched out, closing his eyes and enjoying the soft sheets under his head. But as he rested, his mind whirled with questions about the day. Beside him, Grant was already snoring, so there'd be no tossing ideas around. Not that PJ had any new ones. The only thing he knew for sure about Gilramore was that there was something funny going on, and no one was giving up their secrets easily.

The dinner hour arrived, and Grant woke up the moment he heard PJ creeping toward the door. Together, they walked downstairs, finding a mixed crowd of the farmers from the market and more than a few soldiers sitting around the inn's dining room in clumps. PJ didn't see Orville, nor anyone else he recognized by name, but some of the faces were familiar. He and Grant queued up behind a pair of sunburned farmers, who were discussing whether it was too late to plant the last round of potato crops.

"Riveting conversation," Grant muttered. "Definitely helps us get closer to the attacker."

When they reached the front of the line, the innkeeper, whose name was Wendy, portioned them a smaller helping than the farmers. Grant grumbled, but PJ just thanked her, grateful for another hearty meal and an actual bed—and a chance to make some headway on their investigation.

"PJ! Over here!" Ygritte waved PJ over. As he approached, she scooted her chair to the side, offering him the empty one next to her. "Have a seat. You look like you're in need of a friend."

"You aren't wrong," PJ said, plopping down next to her. "Is Orville coming?"

"Nah. He's at home to eat with his husband." She beamed at him. "But he did tell me to keep an eye out for you and make sure you got a seat. It can get pretty cutthroat in here when it gets busy." She nodded across the room toward Grant, who'd sat at a table of queen's soldiers and was the only one happy about it. "Your friend's got himself in with the wrong crowd."

"He'll figure it out eventually," PJ said mildly.

"You seem to have enough sense to know who to help and who to leave alone," Ygritte said with a smile. "Though can't say I was too disappointed to see Quentin get it today."

PJ stuffed his mouth full of root vegetables and nodded. This farmer seemed chatty, and the more she talked, the more he could learn.

"I heard Orville telling you about the Pearlwinds —the witch family. They were friends of mine. I never thought it was right what Quentin did to 'em, bringing the queen's folks to town and telling 'em where to find the magical folks. Never mind he's got minotaur blood from his father, but—"

"Minotaur?" PJ blanched. He certainly hadn't seen *that* in the soldier. "I guess he got the human half."

"Too right. Lucky for him."

"The Pearlwinds and Quentin were the only magical folks around here?" PJ said. "No one else?"

She nodded, spearing a bright orange carrot. "We were lucky. I heard whole towns of magical people got wiped off the map. Then the queen stuffed 'em full of her own people."

"That kind of happened here, didn't it?" PJ said. "Orville said there wasn't much to this place before the registrars—and that it was Byron who brought them here."

Her face darkened. "Yeah. He's just as bad as Quentin, if you ask me. They both turned their back on their own town to suck up to that crowned—" She swallowed. "The Wersts were a respectable family once upon a time. Set up the general store. Got things in from elsewhere. Mildred Werst still lives in town, you know. Watches the littlest one of that brood while her parents work."

PJ nodded. He hadn't met her yet. "We had dinner with the Wersts the first night we were here."

"Oh, I bet that Abigail regretted that, you being *special* as you are."

"I have no idea what you're talking about," he replied with a neutral smile.

"Mm. Yeah. I saw what you did." She winked at him. "But in any case, Abigail's probably the most loyal person to the queen in this town. I bet you half the reason the queen's likeness is still up is because Abigail demanded it."

"Not the mayor?" PJ asked.

"Who knows if Mary's still really the mayor, you know? With all the upheaval…." She nudged him under the table. "You didn't really work for Dag

Flanigan, did ya?"

PJ shrugged, not wanting to confirm nor deny, even though Ygritte had some anti-queen sentiments. "Any theories on who hurt Quentin? Or who might *want* to hurt him?" He paused, looking around. "Maybe one of the farmers has a vendetta you might've heard about?"

She eyed him. "Are you suggesting it was one of us?"

"Not at all. Just asking questions," PJ said, quickly stuffing more food into his mouth. If no one else had magic on their own, he couldn't rule out that one of the locals might've purchased something, the way Grant's aunt had purchased the curse on Vicky.

"I don't know how it was in *your* town," she said, sounding a bit annoyed. "But here, everyone in town was tested, and tested, and tested again. Couldn't sneeze twice without a soldier showing up at your door to prick your finger. If anyone had a drop of magic, they would've been shipped off. Quentin avoided it by selling out the Pearlwinds and slapping on those iron bangles, of course."

"It seems like it's been a hard time."

"Well, on the contrary." She chuckled. "Having so many new faces in town was a boon for all of us farmers. We went from having to take our wares hours out of town to having a thriving market steps from our front doors." She pushed the remnants of her dinner around the plate. "The inn's been nice, too. Haven't made myself dinner in ages. Wendy's a good cook, and the company's even better—as long as you steer clear of the queen's folks."

"They aren't really her folks anymore, are they?" PJ asked.

"Don't say that too loudly," Ygritte said. "There were those who took the news well, of course. But others…well. Some of 'em had the good sense to skedaddle as soon as they realized they didn't have the queen's protection anymore. Safer to disappear."

"Like Burt Gibbons?" PJ asked, hoping he sounded innocent.

"Mm. Not sorry to see *him* go, I tell you."

"Why?"

"He was ornery. He never thought the king's soldiers should've been forgiven, and he let them know it, too. I'm not surprised he left town as quickly and quietly as he did." She grunted, nodding to the door. "Wish more of 'em would take the hint."

PJ followed her gaze to a loud group of soldiers walking in, led by a man who swaggered like he owned the place. He sauntered up to a table of farmers and jumped as if he were going to attack. Those seated scrambled up, leaving their plates and tankards behind, and the new soldiers sat, laughing to themselves as Wendy quickly gathered the dirty dishes.

"Who's that?" PJ asked, though he was pretty sure he knew the answer.

"*Carl* and his merry band of monsters," Ygritte said, pushing away her plate. "You should probably get out of here. Those idiots like to cause trouble sober, and they won't take kindly to folks who are *special*, you know?"

"I'd like to see what they do," PJ said, mildly.

"Your funeral," she said, rising. "Assuming you aren't beaten to a pulp this evening, will you be loitering in the town square again tomorrow?"

PJ shrugged. "Doesn't look like we're going to solve the mystery tonight."

Ygritte bade him farewell, and PJ remained where he was, watching the room as he picked at his meal. The loud bullies were even louder now, their thick limbs swinging wildly as they told raunchy and inappropriate stories. Ygritte wasn't the only one they'd scared off, as the formerly crowded dining room thinned out as the minutes wore on.

"You ready to head back upstairs?" Grant asked, coming to sit next to PJ. "I didn't get anything outta anyone."

PJ smirked. "Hope nothing else breaks, because that means I won our bargain."

"Oh, who remembers that?" Grant rolled his

eyes.

"I do," PJ said with a pointed look. "I had a nice conversation with Ygritte just now. She confirmed a few things and gave me more to think about. And we can consider her a new friend, too, which counts for something."

"I don't think that qualifies as winning," Grant said. "We can call it a tie."

A loud guffaw broke out at the table with the ruffians, and Grant shifted uncomfortably.

"I'm getting the sense things are about to go downhill quickly in here," he said, keeping his voice low. "We should probably head upstairs."

As much as PJ wanted to say otherwise, Grant was right. The room had all but cleared out now—and one of the goons was staring at them. When he met PJ's gaze, he cracked a smile, like he was about to make his move.

But the door opened, and Quentin walked in, realizing too late that he'd become the focus of the bullies. They smirked at one another, sharing knowing looks of glee as they sat back in their chairs.

Quentin, for his part, bravely crossed the room to make himself a plate, perhaps hoping if he sat down and didn't meet their gazes, he could avoid their scorn.

"Heard you were attacked by *awful* butterflies

today, Quentin," the man PJ assumed was Carl said. "However did you survive such a *devastating* assault?"

"It was nothing," Quentin said, looking like he was warring between his empty stomach and his instinct for self-preservation.

"Was it?" Carl continued, leaning back in the chair so far that it creaked and groaned under his weight. "You were crying like a baby. Had to be helped up." He smirked at the rest of his table. "Like a weakling. Don't you have *magic*? It's legal now, you know. You could take off those iron bangles and show us how very *strong* you are."

The rest of the group cackled.

"Why don't you go stand watch in the town square, see how you like it when they attack *you*." Quentin's face flushed.

"It's probably a good thing you were relegated to shoveling horse dung behind the armies," another man chimed in.

"Yeah, the queen hired you to work for her because the king said you were too useless!"

"He probably couldn't even fight off a fairy—"

"All right, all right," Wendy said, walking into the center of the room between the table and Quentin. "You lot calm down, or you won't be welcome here again, understand?" She pointed at the burly man in the center. "Especially you, Carl. I hear you've been keeping iron by your bed, in case one of your *wards* decides to pay you a visit and repay you for all the kindness you've shown them over the years."

Carl's eyes flashed, and Wendy, for all her bluster, flinched. "I don't think you want to cross me again, Wendy. I'll eat where I please and say what I like, understand?" He rose and towered over Wendy.

The hair rose on the back of PJ's neck as he readied himself to step in. Not that he was any match for the soldier, height-wise, but the dragon within wouldn't stand for injustice like that. Even if Wendy had been frosty to them at first.

Not yet.

The dragon's voice echoed in his mind, taking him completely out of the room. PJ's gaze went to Grant, who clearly hadn't heard the command, then back to the scene. In the few moments he'd been distracted by the dragon, Wendy had found the upper hand—in that Quentin's desire for self-preservation had won out and he'd left.

"You three just eat your food," Wendy said, her voice a little shaky. "And we'll have no more trouble."

"Get that ale, and there won't *be* any more trouble."

"And that's our cue to leave, Peej," Grant

muttered. "I don't want these idiots zeroing in on you."

Neither, apparently, did the dragon. PJ was still unnerved every time the voice in his head decided to share his opinion, especially as there wasn't any rhyme or reason to it. "How are we supposed to get back upstairs?"

"Mm. Good point." Grant thumbed toward the front door, which was closer. "Maybe we wait until they're good and drunk then sneak by them."

PJ didn't disagree, and thankfully, the gang was too preoccupied by their incoming tankards to notice PJ and Grant slipping out. Once the door had closed behind them, Grant let out a sigh of annoyance.

"Glad we didn't have people like that back home," he said. "Only ruffians in Pigsend were—"

"Us," PJ said with a laugh. "Wendy seemed like she could handle it, though."

"Kinda interesting that they hate Quentin," Grant said thoughtfully. "I mean, they all fought for the same side."

"Maybe they don't think he really did, seeing as he's half minotaur," PJ said. "The human half, obviously."

"His attitude is definitely the bull half," Grant said. "Well, Peej, we've got a few hours to spare. Shall we take a stroll up to the apple orchards and get dessert—"

"Absolutely not," PJ said. "We should go check on Wendy. Thank her for her hospitality."

"Do we have to?"

"You catch more flies with honey than—" The dragon perked up in his mind a moment before the sound of someone screaming reached his ears. It wasn't coming from inside the inn, but once again, the dragon took control, moving PJ's feet as it drew him closer to the attack, around the back of the inn.

Where he found Wendy, surrounded by those same golden butterflies.

CHAPTER TEN

Having gone through this scenario earlier in the day, PJ was less surprised when the dragon took over, though it still felt weird to have something else controlling him. He walked up to the innkeeper, opening his mouth to exhale the dragon's breath, and scattered the spell. As it dissipated, there was that same *intention*. Someone was just as mad at Wendy as they were at Quentin, and they wanted her to know it.

But who?

The dragon went back to sleep in his mind, and PJ became aware of Wendy, panting loudly at his feet as she clutched her apron and stared at the sky. He offered his hand to help her out of the dirt, but she swiped it away.

"Get away from me!" she bellowed.

"They're gone," PJ said, kneeling to her level. "Promise. You're safe now."

She inhaled and exhaled, looking around. "I d-don't even know what happened. I was just…" She lifted a shaky hand to her head. "I didn't even think butterflies could *do* something like that!"

"Let's get you inside," PJ said.

"Maybe not *inside*-inside," Grant said. "As Carl and his fellow goons are probably still drinking."

"Then the kitchen," PJ said, extending his hand again. "Come on. It's all right."

This time, she timidly took his hand and allowed him to pull her upright. She leaned into him as he helped her back through the yard to the kitchen door. The goons were, in fact, still loudly drinking, but at least there was a chair next to the fire that PJ settled Wendy into gently.

"Can you find the kettle?" PJ asked. "And maybe lock the kitchen door?"

"Why do I gotta—" Grant started then wisely stopped when PJ gave him a look—one that might've had a little dragon behind it. "Right. Kettle. On it."

While Grant tended to that, PJ turned his

attention to Wendy, making sure her injuries weren't too severe. Like Quentin, there were little nicks and cuts on her face and hands, and her pinned-back hair had come loose, but other than that, she was in good health.

"When I heard what happened to Quentin..." she began quietly, "I thought, butterflies? But those aren't ordinary butterflies." She turned over her hands and arms, inspecting the damage to her clothes. "I've never experienced anything like that before in my life."

"Someone's got a vendetta for sure," PJ said gently.

Before she could respond, Mary burst through the back door, followed by Grant, who had a full kettle sloshing in his hands.

"Wendy? Oh, goodness, you poor thing." She hurried over, all but pushing PJ away to take his spot, and gently cradled Wendy's hand in hers. "Are you all right?"

"How'd you...?" PJ asked.

"I live next door," Mary said. "I heard the screaming and saw it all from my back window. Came over as quickly as I could." She patted Wendy on the hand. "What happened? Spare no detail."

"I was out getting water for the dishes," Wendy said, staring off into the distance. "Then, this flock of...well, bugs came out of the sky and started attacking me." She shivered. "I didn't see anyone around—"

"Did they come from the east?" PJ asked.

"Yes." She looked up at him with watery eyes. "Whatever you did… Thank you. *Thank you*."

"It's what we're here for," PJ said, glad to see something other than disdain on her face. "Now, are you feeling up to answering a few questions?"

She let out a shaky breath and nodded.

"Is there anyone who might be angry with you?" PJ asked. "Someone who'd want to hurt you?"

"Gosh, no one," Wendy said with a shiver as she looked at Mary.

"Our town isn't that kind of town," Mary said definitively. "Everyone gets along."

"Clearly not," Grant said dryly.

Mary bristled, but Wendy looked honestly confused. "I don't know a single person who has a quarrel with me. Maybe they do and I don't know it, but—"

"Have you turned anyone away from the inn recently?" PJ asked.

"What?" She frowned. "What do you mean?"

"Something Byron told us when we first arrived," PJ said, looking between the two women. "That you'd turned away magical people who were looking for a room."

"Well, I hardly think that warrants someone

sending monstrous little creatures to attack me," Wendy said, sharing a look with Mary. "I'm allowed to decide who gets to sleep under my roof, am I not? Why would—"

"You're absolutely within your rights to deny anyone," Grant said, with a melodramatic nod of agreement. "Absolutely no question—"

"But it would provide a motive," PJ finished. "You and Quentin were both targets of the same magical person. If we're looking for a common thread, it might be someone who's got a vendetta against the queen."

"Certainly no one who lives here," Mary said.

"Which is why I was asking about who she's turned away from the inn," PJ finished. "Maybe they had a run-in with Quentin, too. Goodness knows he tried to shoo us out of town when we first got here."

Wendy opened and closed her mouth. "Well, I did..." She cleared her throat. "The last *magical* creatures who came through are long gone. It was over a week ago that they stopped in. And they were most understanding about our policies. I can't imagine they'd wait around a week *then* cause problems."

"How does that line up with the attack on Burt Gibbons?" PJ asked Mary.

She flushed, especially when Wendy gave her a

sideways look. "Well before."

"Are you from this town originally?" PJ asked Wendy.

Wendy shook her head. "Not originally. My husband—rest his soul—had been assigned here as a registrar and passed away a few months after we'd gotten settled. The town had just finished building this inn, and they needed an innkeeper. I needed a job and a place to live."

"How long ago was that?" PJ asked.

"Four years, maybe?" She shook her head. "After the town was already a registrar center."

So not responsible for uprooting a family of magicals. "Did you know about the Pearlwinds?"

Mary did a double-take. "W-what about them? They're gone. I told you."

"Yes, but people who were gone are coming back," PJ said. "Can you think of any reason one of the Pearlwinds might want to hurt you, Wendy?"

"They're *gone*," Mary said, throwing her hands in the air. "I promise you."

"We need all the facts if we're going to figure this out," PJ said, hoping he sounded patient and not annoyed.

"I never met them," Wendy said with a shake of her head. "But…"

"But?" PJ turned to Mary, who'd pursed her lips tightly.

"Inez Pearlwind had a small charm shop in town." She said the word as if it were a filthy curse. "It was torn down to build the Gilramore Inn."

PJ's brows rose. That certainly sounded like a connection.

"But that wasn't my fault," Wendy said with a shake of her head. "It was already built when I arrived in town. Why would they want to attack *me* for just living here?"

"Maybe they're looking for someone to blame?" Grant offered, shrugging.

"The Pearlwinds were taken away by Her Majesty," Mary said firmly. "I *don't* think it's wise for us to be talking about them. People are already on edge, and if you get them talking about a family of witches who *should've* been…" She cleared her throat. "It'll cause mass panic. We aren't equipped to deal with that right now. It's hard enough keeping the peace when—"

A loud laugh echoed from the dining room just beyond, reminding them that Carl and his friends were still in the front room.

"Why don't I take you upstairs?" Mary said. "We'll, erm…close the dining room early. I'm sure Carl will understand. He's quite reasonable."

Wendy, PJ, and Grant stared at her.

"I'm still mayor," she said, breathlessly. "He'll have to listen to me."

"Why don't we get started on cleaning up in here, then?" PJ said, nodding to Grant, who was shaking his head behind Mary and Wendy. "We can get the dishes done and whatever else needs tidying tonight. You get some rest, and we can talk more in the morning."

"I'd appreciate that, thank you," Wendy said with a grateful smile. "But maybe we could take the back way to my room, Mary. I'd rather not face Carl looking like this."

"Of course," Mary replied, helping her up. "I'll take care of it."

Mary declined PJ's offer to help Wendy to her room, instead insisting on taking her alone. When they were gone, PJ turned to the kitchen, walking toward the sink and grabbing the nearby bucket to take to the hand pump in the back yard.

Grant followed him to the door and leaned against the frame. "Are you really going to clean all these dishes?"

"*We* are going to clean all these dishes," PJ said, walking to the pump. When he put his hands on the handle, a zap of pain ran up his arms and he let out a yelp of pain. He winced and wrung out his hands. "And you get to pump."

Grant scoffed and walked out to the pump. "You think we'll get a silver for this?"

PJ inspected his red hands. "No clue. But it's not very charitable to go to bed and leave this mess for Wendy to clean up."

"She cleans it up every day," Grant said, pumping the water slowly.

"She was attacked, Grant," PJ said, picking up the bucket by the wooden parts and putting it under the pump to catch the water.

"I mean, it was *butterflies*. Can they really do that much damage?"

"*Magical* butterflies," PJ said. "Besides that, technically this should be your job, seeing as you lost our bet."

"I seem to recall it was a tie," Grant said. "And this isn't construction. It's dishes."

"So aren't you so lucky this doesn't require slinging a hammer?" PJ replied, putting a second bucket under the stream of water when the first one was full. "You'd be doing dishes if you went back to Pigsend. At least here, we have a puzzle to figure out. One you can use to woo potential girlfriends in the future."

"*Who's attacking the citizens of Gilramore with butterflies?*" Grant said with a mock tone. "My curse story is better than this."

"We'll see." PJ picked up the first bucket and carried it back into the kitchen, where he poured it into the sink along with some soap. He grabbed the first of the stack of dishes—a cutting board—and scrubbed as well as he could.

Grant sidled up next to PJ and took the clean board from him, drying it with a towel. "So when's this coin supposed to show up? Because this is *not* my idea of a good time."

"When the task is done, I suppose." PJ wasn't *really* in it for the money, though it would be nice to make enough to pay for their meals. His true goal was to earn some brownie points with Mary in the hopes she'd be a bit more open to telling him what was going on. There was something about this town she wasn't telling PJ—either because she didn't want him to know or she didn't want word getting out. "What do you reckon we should do next?"

"Not sure, honestly," Grant said. "That witch angle seems promising, though. Though if I were betrayed the way it sounds like they were, I wouldn't want to come back."

"They weren't *betrayed*," Mary announced from the doorway. "They were simply arrested for being in violation of the queen's laws. No more, no less."

PJ could've argued that there was much more to it but instead asked, "How's Wendy?"

"She's fine," Mary said with a nod. "The tea calmed her down considerably, but I'm sure she'll be a little nervous to walk outside tomorrow." She inspected the cutting boards. "These are still dirty."

"Just the first rinse," Grant said, though PJ had considered them done already.

"Well, we now have three victims," Mary said. "And to my eyes, it doesn't look like you two are any closer to figuring out who's behind it. Seems like you're just in town to rebuild after the damage is done."

PJ dunked the heavy pot into the sink—grateful it had wooden handles—and turned to Mary, leaning against the wash basin. "It seems we're not getting the full story. You failed to mention the Pearlwinds in our first meeting—or that they have a reason to attack Quentin. And now there's a connection with Wendy, too."

"That's hardly a connection," Mary said, waving them off. "And I didn't mention it because that family is gone."

"People are coming back," PJ said.

"If you're curious, you can head over to their family lands," Mary said, dismissively. "No one moved in after they were taken. I'm sure it's fallen into disrepair. But you can see for yourself if you're so curious."

"Have you gone to check?" PJ asked.

"Well, no, but..." Her cheeks reddened. "Surely, we'd have seen them on the roads. Or they'd have come to town. Or..."

"Or you're scared of what you'll find if you go,

so you're sending us instead," Grant finished for her.

Mary scowled at him. "Mind your words, young man, or you'll find yourself escorted to the edge of town by our soldiers. Carl would love to—"

"Then who'd solve your butterfly problem?" Grant retorted. "Because it doesn't look like you're doing a great job of it."

"All right, all right," PJ said, when Mary took a step toward them. "Tensions are high. We'll go check out the witch's house tomorrow and make sure nobody's hiding out there. In the meantime, *please* think about what else could connect our victims. Right now, the only thing I can see is that they all lived in Gilramore—and that doesn't help us narrow down our suspect list. None of the victims except Quentin has magic, right?"

"Well, that's an overexaggeration." Mary rolled her eyes. "I wouldn't say he has magic, more that he has magic in his lineage."

"Did Burt Gibbons have magic, too?" PJ asked. "And also wear iron bangles?"

Mary opened and closed her mouth. "N-not that I'm aware of."

"And Wendy? Any magic there?"

"Certainly not," Mary said.

"Though I bet there's plenty of magic in the soil from the charm shop that was here before the inn, right?" Grant said. "What if the butterflies are drawn to sources of magic? Where was Burt attacked?"

"Outside his home, which has no connection to the Pearlwinds or magic whatsoever," Mary said.

"I already checked there," PJ said. "While you were, erm, resting. All I found were half-planted flowers."

Grant tapped his finger against his chin. "There's not a magical river underground, is there?"

"Magical...?" Mary shook her head, as if they were discussing bawdy topics instead of trying to unravel a mystery. "As I've told you time and time again, this is an upstanding town that was the pride of Her Majesty's service. There's no magic, or magical people, or magical families, or magical *rivers* or whatever you say anywhere in this town." She cleared her throat and lifted her chin. "Whatever is attacking our citizens is clearly an *outside element*."

"Okay, well... Where is it?" Grant asked. "The only outside element is us, and it ain't us."

"That *is* the question, isn't it?" Mary said before looking around the kitchen. "You're really going to tidy all this up? And what? Barter for a free night?" She crossed her arms. "You didn't ask Orville for a single coin, but you went through all that effort to fix his farm stand. Why?"

"We already paid for tonight," PJ said, with a warning look at Grant to keep his mouth shut. "As for why I helped Orville… He looked like he could use a hand. Not his fault Quentin destroyed his stand, you know? Didn't want him to be without a place to sell his wares for too long, so we got it put back together."

"Mm." Mary didn't look like she believed him but didn't argue, either. "Well, if you're sure you want to tackle all the dishes, there are plenty more in the front room. Carl and his friends will drink until they can't see straight, and you'll have to ensure they don't sleep on the floor of the inn."

"I thought you were going to—"

"You two seem to have a handle on it," Mary said, walking to the back door. "Have a good evening."

Neither PJ nor Grant wanted to interrupt the raucous conversation happening in the inn's dining room, so they tackled the dishes, wiped the counter, swept the floors, washed the windows, and even watered the small herbs Wendy kept in her window. All the while, the conversation in the dining room grew louder and louder.

"I suppose they're helping themselves to ale," Grant said.

Finally, there was nothing left to clean, and the boys wanted to go to bed, so PJ, the braver of the duo, walked out to deal with the soldiers. But when he stepped into the dining room, he found them asleep.

"Well, that's one way to solve the problem," Grant said, peering over PJ's shoulder. "Did you use your dragon-y powers—"

"No, Grant," PJ said with a sigh. "We should probably do something with them. Mary said they aren't allowed to sleep on the floor."

"What do you think Wendy does?" Grant said, already halfway to the stairs. "They're huge. She can't pull them by herself."

"Grant…"

"Just leave 'em. I'm sure they'll wake up and lumber out on their own accord before Wendy gets up in the morning." Grant yawned. "Besides that, we got bigger fish to catch in the morning. And I need my beauty rest."

PJ woke the next morning feeling well-rested and warm—until he realized Grant was poking around in his bag. "What are you doing?"

"We didn't get paid last night," he said, pulling out PJ's spare shirt and turning it inside-out. "All that work to clean up the inn and not even a *silver* from the amulet. What gives?"

"I don't know," PJ said, having not given it a second thought. After they'd finished with their work, he'd gone right up to bed to enjoy as many hours as he could in a soft bed. "But we don't need it right at this moment, do we?"

"You don't. But I don't like working without

getting something in return." Grant picked up one of PJ's boots and turned it over. "I mean, cleaning all that up took longer than fixing that farm stand, didn't it?"

"Not really," PJ said with a laugh. "Calm down, Grant. I'm sure there's a reasonable explanation. Maybe it'll come later."

Grant made a noise as he threw down PJ's things and sank onto his own bed. "I think it's time you write the grannies. They really did you a disservice by not telling you everything you needed to know. And I bet you a silver they'd probably tell you to pull your head out of your butt and move on from this town, eh?"

PJ clicked his tongue. If he were being honest with himself, that was a large part of why he *hadn't* written to them yet. Not that they were in charge of his every move, but if they told him he was wasting his time, he'd have less reason to stay. But he wanted to stay—he was invested in this town, in the people, and in what in the world was causing them so much trouble. After all, no one else could stop the attacks. And what was the point of having all this magic if he didn't use it to make the world a better place?

"I'll probably pen one tonight," PJ said, putting on his shoes and not looking at Grant. "Ask them if they know anything about butterflies."

"And about the amulet. And why you're hearing

voices. And what the heck you do to stop the butterflies with that breath. And why your eyes turn red. And—"

"I get it," PJ said with a look. "I'm still me, Grant. Just me with a special skill. And an amulet that sometimes feels like it wants to give us a coin or two."

"Well, it'd better spit one out soon, because we've got another night to pay for if we're going to stick around and solve this town's problems," Grant said. "Unless your farm friends have a few spare bedrooms they'd let us sleep in."

PJ rose and stretched, looking out the window at the morning light and feeling optimistic. "I'm sure Wendy's going to be in a fine humor this morning. She'll probably let us stay for free, seeing as we did clean up and save her from the butterflies."

But when they got downstairs, they found a decidedly *bad*-humored Wendy waiting behind her front desk. Far from grateful, she glared at the two boys, acting as if they were responsible for the cuts on her face.

"Erm, good morning," PJ said, clearing his throat. "How did you—"

"Checkout was an hour ago," she said without letting him finish. "I'm behind schedule changing those sheets and getting them washed. Unless you think you're going to stay another night, in which case, I'll need payment now."

PJ cleared his throat nervously, ignoring the smug look from Grant. "We haven't decided yet. Remains to be seen if we figure out who attacked you."

Wendy narrowed her gaze, as if being reminded that she needed saving was offensive. "Well, until you *do* decide, be sure to clear all your things out of that room so it can be available to someone else. I'm not running a charity here, you know?"

"Come now, Wendy," Grant said, sauntering over to her and flashing that same smile. "Surely you can give us a *bit* of grace, considering what we did for you yesterday?"

"You mean, making a mess of my kitchen? Leaving dishes all over the place? Letting Carl and his friends sleep on the floor of my inn? 'Bout had a heart attack when I woke up this morning. Should've just done it myself—"

"The kitchen was *spotless*," PJ said, anger rising in his chest. "And as for Carl—"

"It's not our fault he's a big lug," Grant said.

"Regardless, I had my work cut out for me this morning," she said, avoiding their gaze. "So no, I don't feel like I owe you a *thing*."

Grant gave PJ a look that clearly said, *Told you so.*

PJ chewed on his tongue, working the anger out before he said (or did) something he regretted. There had to be a reason for the sudden shift in personality —she'd clearly been grateful the night before. And he was sure even waking up to a dining room full of sleeping oafs wasn't the cause.

"We're just glad you're okay this morning," PJ said, with some effort. "We're going to continue our investigation, so if you have anything else you want to share about last night, or who might want to hurt you—"

She leveled a glare at them. "Nope. Ain't got nothing to say to you."

"Then who are you going to talk to?" Grant asked, looking around. "Quentin? He was as scared of 'em as you were—"

Wendy's nostrils flared, and Grant wilted under her glare. "It's two gold coins for you tonight, if you want to stay," she said. "And it'll be three if you stay too late again tomorrow. Now get out of my inn."

"What crawled up her butt?" Grant said as they left the inn. "What happened to gratitude? You saved her. She was all weepy and shocked yesterday. Now she's acting like you're the one who did it."

"Something's fishy," PJ said. "I—" He stopped abruptly, as a pair of soldiers blocked their path. They weren't the same bullies as the night before, but they seemed menacing enough. "Can we help you?"

"What's your business in town?" the one on the left asked.

"We've been hired by the mayor to investigate the butterfly attacks," Grant said. "Now get out of our way so we can do that."

"You aren't welcome here," the other soldier said.

But they moved, leaving PJ and Grant even more confused. As they ventured out into the square, PJ couldn't help but notice every person who'd worked for the queen was watching them with wary eyes. Even Quentin, who was back at his post, had apparently forgotten that PJ had saved him from a swarm of butterflies not a few days before and seemed suspicious of them.

"Are you absolutely positive you want to stick around?" Grant asked under his breath as they walked by another trio of soldiers glaring at them. "Because I'm starting to get the feeling no one really wants our help. And this town is getting more unfriendly by the moment."

"Which is why I've been focused on making friends," PJ said, spotting someone waving at him from across the square. "C'mon."

Ygritte was setting up for the day, and she, at least, was happy to see PJ. She offered him and

Grant a shiny red apple each—free of charge—which PJ smugly pocketed while Grant scowled and munched on his.

"Do you know why everyone seems to hate us this morning?" PJ asked, as another pair of soldiers glared at them. "Because yesterday felt a little different."

"Mary Helmsberg was telling them to keep an eye on you," Orville said, walking over from his stand. "She told us there was another attack—Wendy got it, this time."

"She did," PJ said. "It was a good thing we were there eating dinner—"

"Or a bad thing, if you ask Mary." Ygritte bristled. "Because she's now whispering that *you* two are the ones responsible."

"That's preposterous," PJ said. "Mary told us herself she doesn't suspect us."

"Well, she's certainly telling other people something else," Orville said. "Don't know why. You must've spooked her last night. Doesn't seem like she wants you to solve the butterfly problem anymore, does she?"

"Which is odd in and of itself," Grant said, returning a glare from a soldier. "The only thing we got into last night was—"

"A conversation about the Pearlwinds," PJ said slowly. "And if anyone else had any magic around these parts."

"Oh, well, that'll get her up in arms, for sure," Ygritte said with a firm nod.

PJ looked around the square, the puzzle pieces falling together in his mind. Something about their conversation yesterday had spooked Mary to the point where she wanted them to feel unwelcome, perhaps to even to leave. She'd clearly spoken to Wendy about upping the price of their room. Her attitude had completely shifted when PJ had mentioned the magical river.

"Well, then, we can ask you about it," Grant said, getting closer to the farm stand.

"If you're all right with answering, that is," PJ added quickly. "Don't want to get you in trouble."

"We're as boring as a potato," Orville said. "Go on. What do you want to know?"

"Apparently, Burt Gibbons was attacked the day before Quentin was," PJ said, lowering his voice. He hadn't wanted to tell anyone about the first attack, but if Mary was going to turn the town against him, he really didn't have a choice. "Same thing. Butterflies."

"Ah, that explains why he just up and disappeared," Orville said with a chuckle to Ygritte.

"Can you two think of anything that could connect Wendy, Quentin, and Burt?" PJ asked.

"I wonder if that Carl guy has anything to do

with it," Grant said. "He harassed both Wendy and Quentin yesterday."

"Carl's a bully," Ygritte said. "Got too much time on his hands. Besides that, I'm pretty sure he's actually *petrified* of anyone with real magic—especially with his history of harassing kingside soldiers. Quentin's just got…well, nothing to write home about, anyway."

"We're going to check out the Pearlwind house today," PJ said, changing the subject. "Know where we could find it?"

"Oh, aye." Ygritte nodded. "But you won't find anything there. Doubtful you'll even *find* it." She shook her head. "Always kind of troublesome to get to, even before the queen's folks arrived. They were quite secretive. Didn't like their neighbors to know too much about what they were up to."

"But they're gone, so…?" Grant said.

"Magic lingers," Ygritte said. "Or so I hear. Lots of anger and resentment on that land. I'm sure it's turned into something awful by now."

Grant shared a dubious look with PJ. "How can land be angry?"

"How much do you know about witches?" Ygritte asked with a knowing smile.

The boys shrugged.

"Well, to begin with, there are more flavors of magic than there are stars in the sky." Ygritte chuckled. "Now, a witch's magic is pretty closely tied to the earth. They tap into the water and air and leaves and whatnot, and that's how they do what they do."

PJ nodded, though he didn't quite follow what she was saying.

"So you have a family of witches that's lived generations on the land, then you suddenly take 'em away. Traumatic, too. Soldiers in iron bangles showing up and yanking 'em outta their beds—or so I hear. The land would probably be pretty angry about that. So…" She shrugged. "I'm just sayin' to be careful. You might get more than you bargained for if you get too close."

"Well, good thing we know how to handle all that," Grant said, throwing an arm around PJ and punching him lightly in the arm.

~

Ygritte gave them instructions, and they set off down the forested road. The Pearlwind property was situated right next to the Wersts' property, and PJ couldn't help but wonder how staunchly anti-magic Abigail might react to such knowledge. But as they found the overgrown bush with the bright purple flowers that marked the entrance to the Pearlwind property, there didn't seem to be any road or house or even a path. Just a thick forest that seemed almost impossible to walk through.

"This is probably what Ygritte was talking about," PJ said, rubbing his chin. "There's got to be some kind of magic protecting it."

Grant walked up to the forest and touched the thick underbrush cautiously. "What do you think would happen if we took an axe or something to it? Do you think we'd get sucked into a witch's hex and our eyeballs would fall out of our heads?"

PJ turned to him. "What?"

"I mean, just trying to cover all the possibilities," Grant said, looking at his fingers nervously. "I like my eyeballs where they are."

"I don't think that would happen," PJ said. "But, just in case, let me go first. Stay here."

PJ stepped off the road, pushing aside the underbrush to clear a path. There was *definitely* magic here. So much so that it surprised him the queen's people hadn't stamped it out, being just down the road. Though they might not have even given this place a second look. Had he not known there was something to look for, he'd have just kept walking down the road.

"Grant?" PJ called, looking behind him.

But his friend wasn't visible anymore. All PJ could see was a thick wall of trees in all directions. Even the sun overhead seemed to have disappeared. He hadn't walked *that* far—maybe three or four steps off the road.

He realized with a start that there was something pressing on his skin.

Magic. No wonder Mary was scared to check the house.

If he thought about it too much, the pressure of the magic might suffocate him. He purposefully inhaled and exhaled, if only to remind himself that he could, and closed his eyes, letting the dragon take over. But even the dragon seemed confused. He was right where he thought he was, but he was also somewhere else entirely. PJ opened his eyes and, for the first time, fear crawled up his spine. He'd just assumed his dragon knew everything and would guide him. But if the dragon was confused, and PJ was certainly confused who was left to save him?

"Deep breaths, Peej," he whispered to himself.

He knelt, touching his fingertips to the dirt and leaves. They reminded him he was in a forest, no matter how dark it had gotten. He inhaled the earthen scent of leaves, and water, and magic. Wind cut through the leaves overhead, rustling them loudly and chilling him. He put a piece of a leaf on his tongue, the bitter, dirty taste a shock to his system.

Light returned to the forest floor, like a cloud had moved away from the sun. PJ rose slowly, and there was a dilapidated house before him. He looked behind him, where Grant was still waiting, tapping his foot and staring at the sky, as if waiting for PJ to come back.

"Suppose he can't see me," PJ said.

"No, he can't."

He nearly jumped out of his skin as he turned to find a woman half his height with spiky gray hair and a few missing teeth glaring at him. She carried a large walking stick in one hand and what appeared to be an iron frying pan in the other—and PJ had a hunch either one could be wielded like a weapon if she had a mind to.

"What are you doing on my property?" she snapped.

"I'm PJ Norris," he stammered, keeping his gaze on the woman's hands before bringing it over to her face. "Are you…?"

"Petunia Pearlwind." She grunted, pointing the walking stick at PJ's head. "And I'll ask you again: What are you doing on my property?"

CHAPTER TWELVE

"P-Pearlwind?"

PJ wasn't sure why he was surprised. There was clearly something magical afoot, so it made sense there was a witch living here. But why hadn't anyone in town known? And was this their culprit?

His gaze went to the frying pan in her hand. *Definitely iron.* But he was able to handle iron, too. Maybe she was so powerful it didn't bother her.

"You got cotton in your ears, boy?" she barked. "I asked you a question. What are you—"

"Looking for you, I guess," PJ said, realizing he should probably tell her the truth, lest she hex him or suck him into the ground or whatever else a witch could do to him. "Erm. How long have you been back?"

She eyed him, lowering her weapons and snorting loudly. "Ain't never left."

He opened and closed his mouth. "Y… Wait, I thought—"

"Well, I'm here. What do you want?"

"Are you attacking people in Gilramore with butterflies?" PJ asked, without anything else to ask.

She let out a hoarse bark of laughter. "Oh, boy. That's a new one."

"So…no?" PJ frowned.

"I ain't got a lick of magic," she said with a snort.

"Wait, what?" PJ frowned. That certainly explained the iron. "What do you mean? You're a Pearlwind—"

"By marriage," she said. "My husband was the witch."

No one had mentioned that the Pearlwinds had a nonmagical amongst them; perhaps they didn't think to. "O-oh."

"Goodness, is this interrogation going to take all day?" she barked. "If that's the case, I'm going to sit down. Come on if you like."

PJ followed her, still trying to process the fact that he'd not only found someone in this magical encampment, but she'd been here for six years without anyone in town knowing. Clearly, no one had thought to check on things, else they would've run into her. That, or they'd been deterred by the magical wards PJ had only just managed to get by.

Actually, the more he thought about it, it was probably the wards.

Still, six years of separation from the rest of the world had taken its toll. The house was barely standing, with large portions of the roof caved in. The wood on the floor had all but disintegrated into the dirt, and there were plants growing up and around all the furniture. In the corner, a bubbling spring was spurting water—which Petunia gathered into a banged-up kettle before walking back to set it over the falling-apart hearth. She offered PJ a very rickety chair and took another one, settling with a loud sigh and putting her walking stick over her knees.

"Well?" She surveyed him. "What kind of creature are you?"

"Pardon?"

"You got through my wards. You clearly know a bit about magic, but you aren't one of the queen's people."

"How do you know?" PJ asked.

"You haven't drawn a weapon yet." She eyed him. "And you don't seem to even *have* one. Which tells me you've got something dangerous up your sleeve. Or you're incredibly stupid."

PJ licked his lips, finally shaking himself out of his stupor. "My name is PJ Norris. I've been hired by the mayor of Gilramore to look into a spate of magical attacks that've happened recently, and I wanted to know…if you were…responsible."

As he spoke, her bushy brows knitted together in confusion. "You thought I was responsible? When nobody knew of my existence here?"

"I didn't know what I'd find here, to be honest," PJ said. "I thought it might've been the witches—"

"The witches are long gone," she said, her voice full of sadness. "It's just me and this house here. So no, I haven't been attacking the *fine folks* of Gilramore, no matter how much they might deserve it." She gathered her hands in her lap. "What kind of attack are we talking about? You mentioned something about butterflies?"

"There've been three so far," PJ said with a nod. "Nastier than you'd expect. Whoever's casting the magic is really angry, too."

"I doubt they'd be attacking if they weren't." She sat back and surveyed him. "Who's been attacked so far?"

"Burt Gibbons," PJ started, watching her for a reaction.

Unfortunately, he didn't get any from her.

"Who's that?"

"He was a registrar in town."

"What's that?"

"Boy, you really haven't been in town recently, have you?" PJ muttered. That or she was playing dumb. "The other two were the innkeeper and Quentin Shellman."

At the last name, she broke into a wide smile. "Oh, *Quentin* was attacked?" She let out a gleeful cackle. "How wonderful. Certainly deserved it, the turncoat. Can't say I know anything about the others, but I'm sure they deserved it as much as Quentin." Her glee finally softened as she inspected him. "So what? You work for the queen? Here to arrest me on behalf of the mayor?"

"N-no." PJ shook his head. "You haven't heard? The queen's no longer on her throne. The king's back in power."

Once again, her expression was inscrutable. "News to me."

"Well, magic is legal again," PJ said.

"Not in Gilramore, I'd wager."

"It's..." PJ thought for a moment. "Why doesn't anyone know you're here? You mean to tell me you live five minutes from town, and *no one's* seen you this whole time? You've never had to go get supplies or food or anything like that?"

She smirked, sitting back. A moment later, the

kettle whistled, but she didn't get up. Instead, a bright green vine slithered across the floor like a snake, crawling up the stone and wrapping around the kettle handle. It lifted it off the fire then carried it over to PJ and Petunia, where another vine was pushing a tray with a teapot and two chipped teacups across the weather-worn table. The first vine poured hot water into the teapot, replaced the chipped lid, then slithered back to the dark recesses of the room.

What if it's the land?

PJ looked around. It certainly looked like an awful place to live, with the holes and the nature coming in, and all of that. But as he stared at the cabinets directly to his left, they shimmered slightly, as if they were covered by some kind of spell. Perhaps this place wasn't as bad off as it seemed— and perhaps there was more to the story than she was willing to tell him.

"That was interesting," PJ said. "I thought you said—"

"The land has magic," she said, as if that were obvious. "It takes care of me." She shifted, her dark eyes drifting to the hole in the roof. "In its own way."

"So you don't need to leave," PJ said. "You get everything you need from the land?"

"Well, not *everything*. I've had to go without

some things." She shifted, adjusting her threadbare cloak. "Haven't had a nice loaf of bread in an age, and my clothes are getting..." She shook her head. "But it's better than leaving. No telling what I'll find out there."

"The world *is* changing," PJ said. "The king's back in power, of course, but you're right, people are slow to accept it. Especially in Gilramore. We haven't been there long." He realized he was getting off track. "But someone is sending flocks of butterflies to attack people. And it's my job to get them to stop."

"But what if the people getting attacked really deserved it? Hm? What then?"

"There are other ways to resolve disputes," PJ said. "If someone's been wronged, then we can make it right—"

She barked a loud, hollow laugh. "Oh, you really are naive, aren't you?"

PJ frowned and blushed. "I'm not—"

"Do you know what it was like when the queen's people came through?" she asked, and PJ shook his head. "It was an awful, awful night. We were taken." She swallowed, perhaps not wanting to relive every moment of the episode. "They tested me. I'm as normal as a dormouse so they let me go. I came back here. I kept waiting for my family to return, but..."

"They still might," PJ said quietly. "There are magical folks all over the country who are returning from… Well, I'm not sure where they're coming from, but—"

"Not my family."

PJ nodded, resisting the urge to reach across the table to take her hand in comfort. He had a feeling she'd spit at him if he tried.

"I'm so sorry that the queen's people were so heartless," PJ said. "And I know there's no love lost between you and the people of Gilramore." He looked to the left, where another long green vine was slithering across the floor. Perhaps best not to ask the question he wanted to ask just yet. "But I'd like to help you."

"Help me?" She barked a laugh. "How in the world—"

"I can bring you some food. Maybe even…" He glanced at the roof but decided against offering to fix it. The house might get mad that it no longer had access to the sunlight. "Whatever you need. I won't tell a soul in Gilramore that you're here, either. But I can help. I want to help. There's no reason you should be stuck here, especially now that I know about you."

She surveyed him for a long time over the edge of her chipped teacup. PJ was half convinced she'd tell him to leave and never come back, but perhaps she realized he could overpower her wards—or whoever's wards they were—even if she didn't want him to.

"You really want to help an old woman like me?" she asked softly as if the idea were hilarious to her. "Out of the goodness of your heart?"

"It's my job," PJ said, and he meant it. She really had lived a hard life, and if he could do one thing to bring a little brightness into her world, he'd do it. After all, how difficult could it be to bring her food? Even in the town of people who hated him, surely they'd—

Coins *thump-thump-thumped* in his pocket, which bolstered his confidence.

"Well, I suppose… if you insist… But I'm not giving you anything in return," she said, gesturing to the house. "I don't have anything to give."

"I'm not asking for anything," PJ said. "So come on. What do you need? What can I bring that would make your day better?"

"Chocolate chip cookies."

PJ started. "I'm sorry?"

"You asked what would make my day better. Chocolate chip cookies would do the trick." She smirked, her wrinkles bunching up on the side of her face. "Yes. That's all I need. A dozen chocolate chip cookies. Freshly baked, of course."

"Should be easy enough," PJ said with a nod.

"I'll be back in a few hours."

"We'll see." She sat back, smirking as if she knew something he didn't. "We'll just have to see."

~

"Where the heck did you go?" Grant asked as PJ emerged from the wards. They were just as difficult to travel through leaving as entering, and more than once, PJ had gotten lost. But his dragon had a point to focus on—Grant—and eventually, PJ had found the other side, shaking off the lingering effects of the magic.

"Found someone in there," PJ said, shaking his head to clear the rest of the magic from it. He gave Grant the long and short of their conversation, including his new task: to find a fresh batch of cookies to bring back to the old woman.

"She wanted you to bring cookies?" Grant said dubiously. "That seems—"

"The land can get her everything else, I think," PJ said.

"I mean, I hate to repeat myself *again*, but… How is finding a dozen chocolate chip cookies related in any way to finding dragon shifters?"

"It's not, I don't think," PJ said, his cheeks warming.

"So why are you doing it?"

"Because you didn't see her in there," PJ said. "She's alone and miserable. All she has for friends are vines and flowers. And she asked for chocolate chip cookies. It's not like that's hard to find, you know? We just need a bakery. Besides that…" He turned back, sensing; the magic wasn't anywhere around them. "I think she's our culprit."

"I coulda told you that," Grant said. "But how do we stop her?"

"Well, that's the thing," PJ said. "She said she doesn't have magic herself."

"And you believed her?"

"The land is magical," PJ said. "Which makes me wonder…what if the land's feeding off her energy? What if she's built up all this resentment toward the town, and the dam's finally broken, and the land is taking her anger and using it to hurt people who've wronged her family?"

"Is that even possible?" Grant asked. "Land feeding off someone's feelings to wreak havoc? You'd think she'd know she was doing it, too."

"I don't know, the house seemed…" PJ thought for a moment. "It was falling apart, practically. I'm amazed there was still part of a roof on. But the plants served her tea."

"How can a plant serve tea?" Grant asked. "And wouldn't the plant be, I don't know, upset by the prospect of boiling leaves if it's *made* of leaves—?"

"Look, I don't know what to tell you, but I saw it," PJ said. "And it's not outside the realm of possibility that the land, spun up on six years of anger, decided to take matters into its own hands and whip up butterflies into an attacking frenzy." PJ gestured back to the property. "There was *anger* in the magic—and that woman looked plenty angry to me."

"Are you sure you weren't just dreaming?" Grant asked, rubbing the back of his neck. "It all seems kinda far-fetched, you know? And I can't imagine Gilramore not knowing she was right here this whole time. She had to have left sometime, right?"

"Certainly didn't sound like it, but she wasn't being completely truthful. I don't blame her. She didn't even know the queen had been overthrown."

"So what's your plan? Butter up an old woman so she stops attacking the town?" Grant asked.

"I think it's a good start," PJ said. "And either way, she needs help. I mean, I've half a mind to get some wood from Orville and repair her roof."

"You have zero clue how to do that."

"Yeah, well, you don't learn until you try," PJ said. "And you'll be there to help."

"Oh, no." Grant held up his hands. "I tried to follow you into that magical nonsense, and it most assuredly spat me out."

PJ shook his head. "Then at least help me find some supplies for her. I was thinking the cookies, like she asked, but maybe also visiting the apothecary for some herbs and tinctures. She was limping, so maybe she needs something for arthritis." He tapped his finger against his chin. "Or maybe I'll just start with the cookies and see what that gets me."

"And how are you going to pay for all this?" Grant asked.

PJ reached into his pocket and showed Grant the three silvers that had appeared earlier. "See? The amulet agrees it's the right thing to do."

Grant rolled his eyes. "I still say you're wasting your time."

"What would Bev do?" PJ asked. "She served dinner to Etheldra no matter how ornery she was."

"Bev is a saint."

"Bev knows that the way to soften people up is to make their lives easier," PJ said. "I don't think the world's been kind to Petunia these past six years."

"The world hasn't been kind to *us* either," Grant said. "Where are we going to sleep tonight? We don't have enough gold to pay Wendy, who is way overcharging us, by the way. And after we spent hours cleaning and scrubbing her inn, too."

"That's because you expected it," PJ said.

"Not to mention the whole town wants us to *leave*," Grant said. "Including the mayor, who's told all her not-employed soldiers to *keep an eye* on us."

"We have friends in the farmers," PJ said. "And

I'm sure they'll be more than happy to point us in the right direction."

Chapter Thirteen

"Chocolate chip cookies? That's going to be a tall order," Ygritte said with a shake of her head. "What do you need cookies for, anyway?"

PJ wasn't exactly sure what to tell her and Orville without revealing Petunia's secrets. He hadn't actually considered what he'd say if someone asked who they were for—and he purposefully ignored the smug look on Grant's face.

"Just have a hankering. Surely, there's a baker around here somewhere, right?"

"Nope. And we don't get chocolate merchants around here too often," Ygritte said. "You'll probably have to keep walking to the next big city.

Two hours there, two hours back—if you make good time."

PJ frowned. Petunia surely hadn't meant to send him on a quest he couldn't finish, had she? Probably not, as she hadn't left her property, thus she'd have no idea that chocolate was in short supply. It had been a somewhat random request, but he'd chalked it up to her just being lonely and needing a special treat.

"Even Pigsend had a bakery," Grant said, looking around at all the shops in the square with a frown. "And we're a little town, you know?"

"The queen's soldiers only brought things to town that would benefit them," Ygritte said. "Tailors, blacksmiths, that sort of thing. They never appreciated a good pastry."

"Not if it hit them square in the face," Orville said, coming over from his stand to chat. "What are we talking about?"

"Looking for chocolate bars, or chips, or chocolate something," PJ said. "I was hoping there was a bakery I'd missed, but it seems like we're going to have to walk to the next town."

"You know, I think I remember talking with Byron Werst about him having some chocolate," Orville said, rubbing his chin.

PJ snapped his fingers, looking at Grant. "The Werst boys mentioned that, too."

"Why would Byron have chocolate?" Grant asked, suspiciously.

Orville looked around. "Between you, me, and the apples here, I think he's trying on new occupations. He's gotten pretty good at baking bread, and I think he wanted to expand his repertoire. Besides that..." He shrugged. "He's got three young kids. Who wouldn't want to bake them a treat every now and again?"

But PJ snapped his fingers, recalling his last conversation with the boys. "Last I spoke with Benny, Byron hadn't made the cookies yet. Maybe we could convince him to?"

"You want to waltz right back onto their property, especially after Abigail made it *quite* clear you weren't to go near her kids again?" Grant retorted.

PJ scowled, earning a laugh from Orville and Ygritte. "Can't blame her for being careful, especially these days. But, erm..." Orville tapped his nose. "I do know she'll be at the registrar's office for a few more hours, so if you're hoping to avoid her, now's the time to visit the house."

"What's she even doing there?" Grant asked. "Queen's gone. She's out of a job, same as her husband."

"I think she's just looking like she's busy," Orville said with a chuckle. "Trying to maintain some semblance of normalcy for the town and her kids until they figure out for sure what to do. Same as the rest of the unemployed soldiers wandering the town." He nodded to Ygritte. "You know, I actually had Red Barrington ask if I needed help with the harvest last week."

"Really? Red?" She let out a chuckle. "That's surprising."

"Seems like that first missed paycheck is spookin' a few of them."

Ygritte glanced toward the town hall, where Carl and his two favorite goons had found their perch on the front steps again. The other two seemed cut from the same cloth as their leader, with one a head taller than Carl and one with slightly thicker muscles. But it was clear who was really in charge. They'd slept off the previous night's drink and were ready to terrorize the town.

"Not the ones who matter, though," Ygritte said.

"They'll run outta coin soon enough," Orville said with a nod. "They probably have more than most, of course, but they don't spend it like they should. Even they'll have to get a real job."

"Sure wish Wendy would stop serving them," Ygritte said. "Would make dinner time a lot more palatable."

"Why does she put up with them?" PJ asked.

"Cause last time she tried to throw them out,

they broke every table in the inn," Orville said, tapping his nose. "Ruined the dining room. She just got it put back together. I don't think she's going to risk making them angry again."

Probably explained the freshly cut wood smell in the dining room.

"Anyway, what about these cookies?" Grant said, looking at PJ meaningfully. "Even if we get chocolate, then we need sugar, butter, flour, an *oven* —" He ticked off his fingers.

"I have all that at my house," Ygritte said. "You boys get the chocolate, then you can come by my house and bake it there. For *whomever* needs it." She winked. "It's been too long since I've had a good cookie. Be happy to take one or two as payment."

That arrangement worked quite well for PJ, and he and Grant bade farewell to the farmers. He hadn't a *clue* how he was going to ask Byron for chocolate without telling him the whole story about the secret witch living not two minutes from Byron's house, or what he'd do if the former registrar didn't have any chocolate to spare, but before he could consider any of that, he was stopped by a dark shadow that blocked out the sun.

"Oi."

PJ squinted as he tilted his head up. Carl and his two brutish friends stared down at him, forming a veritable wall of ogreish men.

"I think you two've worn out your welcome, yeah?" Carl continued. "Seems like all this magical stuff started when you showed up. Bet it'll stop when you leave."

"It would certainly appear that way, wouldn't it?" Grant said, his voice dripping with casual disdain. "But no, we've just been hired to fix the problem."

"I heard." Carl puffed out his chest menacingly. "Getting some gold outta it, aren't you?"

"If we solve it," PJ said, hoping to bypass the wall and get on their way. He was pretty sure these idiots wouldn't last a second against his dragon, but he didn't want to have to break that out in the middle of the town square, either. "Which we were on our way to do. If you'll excuse us—"

"We can stop it," Carl said, thumbing at his chest. "Don't need strangers around."

"I don't think you can muscle your way into making the culprit reveal themselves," Grant drawled with a sideways look. "Or you would've done it already."

"No, but we've got a *lot* of experience in making magical people tell the truth." He lifted a pair of iron bangles—not unlike the ones Quentin wore— and shook them in front of PJ's face. "What do you think about this, eh? Maybe we slap these on you, keep you from attacking people."

"Feel free." Grant offered his wrists. When Carl sneered at him, Grant snatched the handcuffs out of his hands and made a show of acting like they were hurting him. "Ow. It hurts. Jeez. You really showed me. They're awful."

Carl's lip curled. "You know, when I used to *visit* my soldiers, they'd sometimes have a smart mouth, too. But I told 'em, nobody would care if anything happened to them. They were traitors to the queen, and life was better if they just did what I said." He sniffed toward them. "Nobody in *this* town's gonna care what I do to you, either."

"Mm, yes, I'm sure you were quite the fearsome spectacle," Grant said, toying with the iron bangles. "But unfortunately, we've been hired. So you can sit this one out. Next time a knot of frogs attacks someone, you be sure to handle it." He nudged the bangles back into Carl's hands. "You can scare them off with these, I suppose. Toodle-oo."

Surprisingly, the three oafs let Grant and PJ pass, and soon they were walking the road toward the Wersts' house. PJ kept glancing behind to make sure they weren't being followed, but as soon as they'd left the square, Carl and his bullies seemed to forget them.

"I hope they don't go mess with Orville and Ygritte," PJ said. "They seem the type, you know?"

"Well, if they do, I know a dragon who might be

able to have some words with them," Grant replied with a smirk. "You know, wouldn't it be a twist if that anti-magic buffoon were wielding butterflies?"

PJ turned to him. "What?"

"I mean, he did get into it with Wendy before she was attacked. And he also clearly hates Quentin," Grant continued, the idea obviously hilarious to him. "Could you even imagine that reveal? Not just that he has magic, but magic comprised of *butterflies*? I'm sure he'd get royally roasted by his two friends. He'd be run out of town in embarrassment."

PJ stared at him, somewhat impressed. "Grant, that very well might be our motive."

Grant made a noise. "I sincerely doubt it. He handled those iron bangles just fine. And, as we've been told, the queen's soldiers were all tested. More likely some angry old woman in the forest surrounded by a sentient house."

PJ really did hope it *was* Petunia, because he'd had about all he could take of that Carl and his friends. The less they interacted, the better. "Thanks for taking those iron bangles, by the way. I'm not sure what they would've done to me."

"Probably hurt," Grant said. "See? I told you I'm useful to have around. I can show the world that *we're* not magical."

PJ snorted. "I hope the next town we go to

doesn't hate magic this much." He exhaled as the Wersts' house came into view. "And that Byron remembers just how much he owes us."

With more than a little apprehension, PJ rapped on the front door. Noise echoed from beyond the door before Byron appeared. His shock quickly turned to annoyance. "What are you two doing here?" he asked. "It wasn't enough that you got me in trouble with my wife—"

"But it was enough that we plucked your son from the creek?" Grant said.

Byron slumped against the doorframe. "Well? What do you want?"

"I heard you have some chocolate," PJ said. "There isn't a bakery here, and I need chocolate chip cookies."

The other man stared at them as if he hadn't heard them. "You need what?"

"It's a long story, one I don't want to get into," PJ said. "So yes or no—do you have chocolate, or do I need to walk to the next town?"

"I do, but…"

"Give us the chocolate, and we won't tell your wife about your son skipping school and falling into the creek," Grant said with a sweet smile. "And we'll be square."

Byron opened the door wider with a heavy sigh. "Fine. Come on in."

PJ and Grant looked at each other but followed him inside, keeping their footfalls silent. As soon as they crossed the threshold, the scent of bread hit their nostrils. And when they walked into the kitchen, they found several loaves sitting on the counter.

"You've been busy," PJ said.

"Gotta do something with my free time," he said, not really looking them in the eye. "I was gonna make some chocolate chip cookies to surprise Abby, but we've just been so… It's been hard to find something to celebrate lately." He turned to them, still looking confused. "Why do you need chocolate anyway? Does this have anything to do with the butterfly attacks?"

"Kind of," PJ said. "Better that I don't share all the details until I know for sure, though."

Byron watched him for a moment. "You know, Abby said you told her you'd come to town because you suspected something was off about Benny. Is that true?"

PJ considered how to answer and decided on the truth. "Something cued me to walk toward the river. I thought it might've been Benny, but—"

"I don't think it was Benny," Byron said, looking at the floor. "I think it was me."

"You?" PJ shared a look of confusion—then recognition—with Grant. "Benny didn't just fall in, did he?"

Byron shook his head. "We were also attacked by a flock of butterflies. I don't think Benny saw them—he was close to the edge of the river—but I did." He swallowed. "As soon as Benny fell in, they disappeared. I don't know... I'm not sure..." He took a long breath. "I don't think someone was trying to hurt my son intentionally. I think they meant the attack for me, and in my haste to fight them off, Benny fell in..."

"Why didn't you say anything sooner?" PJ asked.

"I... Well..." Byron said, his cheeks turning red as he rubbed the back of his neck. "I didn't think anything of it, you know? Then Quentin was attacked, and Wendy, and..."

"Burt, your neighbor," PJ said.

He nodded. "I just found out about that last night, when Abby was telling me you'd taken the boys across the yard. I knew he was out of town, but..." He turned to them, looking honestly worried. "You don't think someone's targeting my family, do you? And if so, why? We were always so kind to our soldiers, you know? They'd have no reason to come after us like this."

"I don't think it's related to your job," PJ said. "What do you remember about the Pearlwinds?"

His eyes widened—from shock or something

else, PJ wasn't sure. "They're gone. Why do you ask?"

"Everyone who was attacked had a connection with them," PJ said.

"I don't," Byron said with almost too much force.

"You're the reason the registrars settled here, aren't you?" Grant asked. "You told Abigail to bring the registrar's office here, right?"

"Well, yeah, but that's not..." He cleared his throat. "That's not... The Pearlwinds were taken because they were magical, not because... I mean..." He shook his head, almost trying to convince himself. "They aren't back. It's impossible. And if they were, they'd... I don't think they were the kind of people to want to hurt an innocent little boy."

"You said yourself the attacker wasn't interested in your son," Grant said.

Byron made a flustered noise.

"What about their land?" PJ said. "What do you remember about it?"

"I don't think you can even get off the road these days," Byron said.

"I went to see the house," PJ said. "It's empty."

"Then why'd you—" Byron jumped up, looking like PJ had offended him. "You should've led with that. Here I am worried these witches are back to seek revenge against us—"

"You probably should be," Grant said. "Because Peej thinks the land is taking revenge. Do you think that's possible?"

Byron opened and closed his mouth. Then he shook his head. "There's gotta be someone to wield the magic there. I don't know much about witches, but I know the land was much more alive when they lived there. So no." He reached into the pantry and produced a small bag. "Here's the chocolate. I'm sorry I didn't tell you sooner about my own brush with the butterflies. But now you know everything I do."

"Thank you," PJ said, taking the bag. "You know, all I want is to find the truth. I'm not trying to stir up trouble or get anyone in hot water with their wife. We haven't told her about Benny's fall, and I don't plan to, either. But it's going to be hard to find the culprit if everyone keeps hiding things."

"The Pearlwinds are long gone," Byron said.

"What about Petunia?" PJ asked. "The nonmagical wife?"

He furrowed his brow. "Who?"

"Petunia Pearlwind," PJ said. "Orville was telling me about her, she—"

"There was no one by that name living there," Byron said. "Ever. There was Inez and Venalda and Garrett, but no one by the name of Petunia. And they certainly didn't have any wives who were nonmagical."

"I see." PJ clutched the chocolate. "Must've misheard then. Thanks for this. If I have extra cookies, I'll be sure to bring them by. Maybe there'll be something to celebrate soon after all."

Chapter Fourteen

"You think Petunia gave you a fake name?" Grant asked.

"I don't know why she would," PJ said, holding the bag of chocolate carefully as they made their way down the dirt road from Byron's house. "There's no... I mean, why would she lie to me?"

"To throw you off, maybe," Grant said. "Perhaps she has magic, but she's trying to play herself off as someone without it, so she made up a name. Maybe she's not a Pearlwind at all, you know? Maybe she's just some magical who found a magical haven and decided to squat there until the real owners come back."

"Then why would she have a vendetta against Gilramore?" PJ asked.

"What's to say she does? What's to say we aren't barking up the wrong tree?" Grant said.

"Well?" PJ gestured around them. "You got any brighter ideas? Because right now, this is the only one I have. There's a potentially magical person with plenty of anger living a stone's throw from the town. Seems like a pretty clear-cut answer."

Grant made a noise but didn't respond.

"We'll start with cookies," PJ said. "Then, if she trusts us, maybe we'll see about repairing her roof or getting her a new cloak. Baby steps. If she isn't the attacker, maybe she can help us narrow down who it could be. Two magical heads are better than one."

"If you say so."

They passed through the farmers' market, which had closed for the day. Even so, the square was full of people milling about as if they had nothing better to do, including Carl, who kept PJ in his sights as they crossed from one side to the other.

"He absolutely looks like he's doing his level best to find the attacker," Grant muttered. "You know, I'll bet you a silver that he's just lurking, waiting for us to find out who did it, then he'll try to take credit for it, along with our gold."

"He could try," PJ said. "Somehow, I don't think Mary will believe him."

"Yes, well, he's not out here asking people to hand over bags of chocolate," Grant said. "I mean, really. It's a good thing Ygritte likes you so much that she didn't question who you're baking the cookies for...but she might once we show up in her kitchen. What are you going to tell her?"

"Hopefully, we can avoid that conversation," PJ said.

Grant sniffed as they passed the last of Gilramore proper and headed down the road. "She said she was friends with the Pearlwinds, right? Maybe she knows that Petunia—or whatever her name is—is still there."

PJ'd considered that. He doubted Ygritte would've told them outright about the nonmagical witch hiding in plain sight, but maybe if she trusted them a bit more, everyone could speak more freely. PJ needed someone to stop hiding their true intentions—or he needed his dragon (who'd been awfully silent) to speak up and get some real answers.

He imagined hauling all the townsfolk of Gilramore into the town square, taking off his amulet, and letting the dragon out to yell at them until someone confessed.

One option, for sure. But in the meantime, he'd make an old, lonely woman a batch of cookies and try to brighten her day.

Ygritte was ecstatic to see them—having been doubtful Byron still had chocolate on hand. "You know, children and chocolate, I just assumed they'd found it and eaten it. Goodness knows my own kids would have."

"Are they still in town?" PJ asked.

She shook her head. "No. They had very strong opinions about Her Majesty, and when the queen's soldiers started moving in, they moved out. I hear from them every so often, but not..." She sighed. "Not as much as I like. My daughter's asked me to sell it and move, but I can't imagine being anywhere other than this farm. Even if the town is full of queen's soldiers."

She welcomed them inside her small farmhouse, which was the next plot over from Orville's and full of apple orchards as well as some closer-in berry bushes. The decor inside was aged, but quaint, with embroidered flowers dotting every piece of furniture and curtain. It was, perhaps, the first building they'd seen in Gilramore that didn't have loyalty to the queen plastered over every single wall.

"I wasn't sure when to expect you boys," she said with a chuckle. "But I can get what you need. I've got a recipe around here, too. It's been so long since I've had chocolate. I'm really looking forward to this."

PJ went with her to the root cellar to retrieve the

supplies, and they joined Grant in the kitchen. Ygritte went for the flour first, but Grant stopped her.

"Erm, no. You want to cream the sugar and the butter first," Grant said. "Then add the eggs then the flour and leavening, then the chocolate chips."

Ygritte looked at him curiously.

"My sister's ex-fiancé was a baker back in Pigsend," he said, his cheeks turning red. "I worked for him for a few weeks. He had me make dozens of cookies one day for a big order. That's all."

"Ex-fiancé, hm?" Ygritte said. "Sounds like there's a story there."

Grant, who never missed an opportunity to tell the tale of his sister's curse, entertained Ygritte as he worked on the cookie dough. Ygritte hung on every word, and PJ just smiled through it, glad Grant could be the one running the show for a change. When Grant got to the part about his sister being cursed, Ygritte tutted and shook her head.

"See, that's why we *need* magical folks," she said. "Anyone with any sort of knowledge would've been able to see that there was something wrong. I mean, a dress catching fire? That's quite clearly a bad luck curse."

"Do you know a lot about magic?" PJ asked.

"I mean, I know what I heard from my friends, the Pearlwinds," she said, looking sad as she stuck a spoon into the cookie dough mix and placed it on the large pan. "They were lovely folks."

"Can you tell me about them?" PJ asked.

"Well, Inez, she was the charmsmith. She had a little shop, right where the Gilramore Inn stands now. Of course, the shop had been abandoned for years before, but..." She sighed. "Then there was Venalda, her sister. They were a pair. Venalda would make the charms at the house, you see, and bring them to her sister. They couldn't cast in the same place, or they'd kill each other. They loved each other, but you know...siblings." She nodded to Grant.

"I do know," he said. "I'm sure my sister hasn't forgiven me for leaving university."

"Oh, you were in university?" Ygritte said with a sigh. "Why'd you leave?"

"Well, it's a long story—" Grant started.

"We flunked out," PJ said abruptly. "Our enrollment and housing was predicated on our good grades."

"Ah, well." Ygritte shrugged. "It happens. Sometimes it's not the right place for you."

"So back to the Pearlwinds," PJ said, slowly. "Were any of them married?"

"Nope. Why do you ask?"

PJ blew air between his lips. "No reason."

They fit as many cookies onto the pan as they

could (under Grant's strict supervision), then it went into Ygritte's oven. Fifteen minutes later, the clumps of dough had spread across the sheet into perfect little discs, with glistening brown chocolate that smelled divine. Ygritte could barely wait until they were cool enough to touch, pulling one off the tray and inhaling the scent.

"Ah, yes. This is heavenly." She sat back.

"Maybe Byron will lean all the way into his baking prowess," PJ said with a laugh. "He was making bread when we stopped by his house. Seems like a bakery could do a nice business in this town."

"Now, you know, that's a brilliant idea," Ygritte said. "If you could convince Abigail to let him out of her sight, that is."

PJ looked down at the twenty-four cookies. "We only need a dozen, and I don't want to risk Abigail's ire should she see us at her house." He tilted his head. "Do you think you could take a few over to the Wersts for us? As a thank you?"

"How many are a few?" She winked at them.

"As many as you want to part with," PJ replied.

She made a noise as she scooped some of the cooling cookies into a basket with a soft tea towel. "You know, if these cookies *are* going to the Pearlwinds, do let them know I'd love to see them. Even if they don't feel safe to come out yet… I miss them." She smiled, her eyes filled with sadness. "I swear I won't tell a soul. But it would be such a relief on my old heart to know they're okay."

"I'll be sure to pass that on," PJ said, then quickly added, "If I run into them, of course."

Basket in hand, PJ and Grant crisscrossed the small town once more to bring the cookies to the thick woods that lined the road just outside Gilramore. Petunia (or whatever her name was) hadn't made the wards any weaker, and it was doubly difficult to navigate them with Grant hanging onto the back of PJ's shirt. But PJ had wanted Grant to come, if only so he could see with his own eyes what PJ had—and form his own opinions.

When they finally emerged into the clearing, PJ thought the house looked less dilapidated, but when his eyes adjusted, things were as they'd been before. How Petunia could live in such a dump was beyond him.

"This place looks lovely," Grant said with a frown. "No wonder she's in a bad mood."

"So you believe me about her anger fueling the land, then?" PJ said as the front door swung open, almost falling off its hinges.

"I mean, I don't not believe you, but..." He plastered on a bright smile as Petunia hobbled up to them with a scowl on her face. "Good afternoon,

I'm—"

"I don't care," she snapped. "What are you doing back here?"

"Cookies, as promised," PJ said, offering her the basket.

She actually looked surprised, taking it and picking up one of the small cookies to inspect it. "These are real?"

"Of course they are," PJ said. "We baked them in Ygritte's oven—"

Petunia sniffed the cookie. "Where'd you get the chocolate? There isn't any in Gilramore. It should've taken you hours to get from here to the nearest town and back. Don't tell me you sprouted wings to fly."

Grant made a noise, sharing a brief look with PJ, who answered, "We got it from Byron Werst—"

At that, she made a noise and dumped the cookies on the ground. "If this was touched by the Wersts, I don't want it. And I don't want you coming back onto my property, bringing strangers as you are. I don't know who this guy is, but—"

"What's your real name, then?" PJ asked. "Because no one in Gilramore has ever heard of a Petunia Pearlwind."

The old woman opened and closed her mouth before taking a step toward them, and the hair rose on the back of PJ's neck as magic increased around him. Magic that seemed to come from *her*. "Did you tell those monsters I was here?"

"N-no, of course not," PJ said. "But—"

"Get off my property. I don't want your help, and I don't want your charity." She turned to walk back to her house. "I'm not bothering anyone, and now you've brought the outside world into my house."

"But—" PJ stopped as vines grew up from the ground, encircling his and Grant's ankles. "What the—"

Another set of vines snapped up from the ground and wrapped around their hands, pulling them backward. And before PJ could say another word, they were yanked back into the magical wards then spat out onto the dirt road—right into a puddle of mud.

PJ lifted his dripping face and looked at Grant, who was mad enough to spit fire. "Of all the… That's the *last* time we do something nice for someone. I don't care if we don't get a gold coin—"

"You definitely don't mean that."

"Well, we're only gonna do nice things for people who appreciate it, then," Grant said, pushing himself to sit. "Because *that* was a giant waste of time. I mean, it's one thing to kick us off her property, but to throw those perfectly good cookies on the ground?" He spat mud. "You weren't joking about the house being sentient, though. If you

hadn't told me she wasn't magical, I'd have thought
—"

"I think she *is* magical, though," PJ said, looking at him. "I don't think her name is Petunia, and I don't think that house is as rough as it looks."

"How d'ya figure?"

"It's hard to explain, but when we first arrived… It was like there's a veil or something over the house. I saw the real house for a moment, then…" He sighed. "And just now, that magic seemed to come from her. But we have bigger problems."

"Such as?"

PJ gaped. "Such as if she's the one doing it, I haven't a clue how to stop her from doing it again."

"Well, I for one am *so surprised* a batch of cookies didn't heal the scar of having her entire family ripped from her and taken away by an evil queen," Grant drawled. "And I'm shocked—absolutely shocked—that the witch, or whatever she is, saw through your thinly veiled attempt to manipulate her."

"It's not manipulation, it's…" PJ sighed, pulling the amulet from beneath his shirt. "The grannies made it look so easy. Just travel from town to town, fixing things that go sideways, and when the problems are solved, boom. Off you go to the next town, the next problem. All with a smile on their faces." He turned it over, wishing it had the answers that were eluding him. "They said I'd run into dead ends, but this feels so much more defeating."

"Then why don't you *ask* them if we should stick around or move on, if you won't listen to me?" Grant said. "Write 'em a letter."

"What if they tell me I'm wasting my time, though?" PJ asked, not meeting his gaze.

Grant let out a long breath. "Why are you so invested in this town, anyway?"

"It's my first…I don't know. Magical mystery." He brushed the mud off his arms. "I feel like if I give in now, we're just… We're always going to give up when it gets hard. And we shouldn't."

"People don't wanna be saved here, Peej. And that's gonna happen sometimes, you know?" He pushed himself to stand and helped PJ up. "You're trying your best. That's admirable. But if everyone in town is telling you the same thing, maybe it's time to listen." He held up his hand and counted off his fingers. "The mayor doesn't trust us. The innkeeper is overcharging us. Our one suspect is using magic to kick us off her land. The Wersts don't want to tell us anything. And here we are, just…" He gestured to the mud covering his clothes. "I know you thought you were doing the right thing, but I don't think this is a problem we can solve."

As much as PJ wanted to hold fast, his optimism

was wavering. Even if he was *pretty* sure the woman who'd just thrown them off her property was sending flocks of butterflies to the town, he still had no idea how to get her to stop—either by force or by persuasion. Maybe Grant was right, and the wounds were too deep to overcome with something as paltry as cookies.

"Yeah, okay," PJ said with a defeated sigh. "Maybe it's time to pack it in and leave."

"We'll fix the next town," Grant said. "Promise." He eyed PJ. "*But for now* any chance that amulet coughed up enough gold for us to sleep in a real bed?"

"I know you two aren't thinking of walking into my inn covered in all that mud and muck," Wendy said, not looking up from the potatoes she was peeling in the kitchen. "There's a hand pump in the yard. Use it. Then you can come talk to me about whatever you want to talk to me about."

PJ wasn't in the mood to argue, so he and Grant plodded over to get some fresh water. PJ watched the inn as Grant pumped the water, thinking about what he'd said, and still feeling like a failure for wanting to leave the problems in town unsolved. They washed up in silence, until PJ decided he was clean enough.

"I'll go talk with Wendy," he said. "Maybe we can negotiate her down on price. I'd rather not use all the coins we have to sleep for one night."

"If she's gonna overcharge us," Grant said, "ask her how long to the next town. Maybe she'll be so glad to be rid of us she'll tell you the truth."

PJ nodded and dragged himself back to the inn, dreading the answer to either question. As he opened the door to the kitchen, Wendy glanced up for a brief moment then back down.

"What sort of trouble were you two getting into?" she asked. "I'd hate to see the other guy."

"Trying to save this town that doesn't want to be saved," PJ said, unable to meet her gaze. "How much for a room tonight? And if you say three coins, we're just going to move on to the next town. Maybe they won't be so ungrateful."

Wendy put down the root vegetable and looked at him for a long time. "One gold."

PJ's attention snapped to her. "Really? What happened to three?"

She returned to her potato. "You look like you've had a rough day. Dinner's at six." She nodded to the kitchen counter. "You can put the coin there."

PJ placed the coin on the counter, relieved some of their bad luck was turning. At least they'd have a good night's sleep before moving on. "And do you have a quill and ink I could use? And letter paper?"

"Why?"

"Gotta write home," PJ said. "If that's all right."

She thumbed toward the front room. PJ nodded his thanks and crossed the kitchen, finding the requested items on her front desk. He took a single leaf and the writing utensils and sat at the table, staring at the blank sheet for a long time. So long, in fact, that Wendy came out to sit at her desk, watching him silently. Finally, he realized he could be upstairs lying in bed instead, so he dipped the quill in the ink and wrote.

Dear Grannies,

I hope you're well.

I need some advice. We've stopped in a town that's been plagued by some kind of magical butterfly attacks. I don't think I'm going to find what you sent me to find, but you also told me to do good where possible. But I don't know if I should stay and help when everyone in town seems to think I should butt out. Grant's ready to leave, and I think I am, too, but the job feels unfinished.

Did you run into this sort of thing? How did you handle it?

Eagerly awaiting your response,
PJ

PJ frowned, rereading his letter and hating how that sounded so juvenile. Almost like he was begging his parents to let him go run around town with Grant and Valta back in Pigsend. But it was the truth, as frustrating as it was.

So he folded the letter and wrote on the address he always used for the grannies. He was fairly sure there was some magic involved, because no matter where he was, or where they were, the letters always got to the right place within a day or so—and the response came just as fast. With the letter folded, he walked it over to Wendy, who took it with a tight smile.

"Do you want me to seal it?" she asked.

"If you like," PJ said. "Nothing in there that's newsworthy, in my opinion. Just writing a letter to my grandmothers."

"Post will be by tomorrow," Wendy said, placing it on the corner of her desk. "I'll make sure it gets out."

And probably read it, too. "Thanks."

She tapped her fingers on the counter for a moment. Then she slid two gold coins—including the one he'd just paid her—across the desk.

"What—?"

"I shouldn't have charged you yesterday, either," she said softly. "Not after what you did, saving me from those awful things. And cleaning the kitchen—it was lovely, you know? You two boys didn't have to do that, and you did, and you did a good job."

"Then why…?"

"Mary wanted me to up the rent so you'd leave town," Wendy said, finally meeting his gaze. "She said you were behind the attacks, trying to extort us, but I just don't believe it. You've paid every coin I've asked, and then some, and Ygritte thinks the world of you. Says you're a kind, upstanding young man."

"She did, did she?" PJ smiled warmly. "It must've been the cookies."

"I don't know about that, but she did come in here about an hour before you two dirty gremlins came back. She told me if I didn't offer you a free bed tonight, she'd never eat here again—and she'd get all the farmers to stop coming, too." Wendy chuckled. "That's a real threat, you know? And she's right, anyway. There's no reason to treat you two like you're dangerous when all you've done is be nice."

Thanks, Ygritte.

"I don't know what to... Thank you. We really are trying to help, but..." PJ shook his head. "It's hard to know what the right thing is when no one's telling us the truth. And the mayor's telling us to fix it one minute then encouraging everyone to get us to leave the next."

She tapped her fingers on the counter. "Between you and me, I think Mary's in over her head right now. She became mayor just because of who her brother is—and her sister-in-law. It was probably pretty easy when everyone listened to the queen, you know? If anyone got outta line, Mary could just report them up the chain and they'd be dealt with. But now..."

PJ nodded. "Now everything's up in the air, isn't it?"

Wendy dropped her voice again. "We don't even have a sheriff around here. Quentin's trying to keep the peace, but you saw him with Carl the other night. They just do whatever they want, and there are no consequences. Mary can't very well have them arrested and sent to jail—where are there jails these days?" She sighed. "So they get away with everything."

"Like when they destroyed all your furniture last week?" PJ asked.

She nodded. "Then they showed up the next day, acting like they didn't do nothin' wrong. Meanwhile, I had to shell out ten gold coins to get new furniture made in a rush. Thank goodness Byron's not busy, or I'd have been up a creek." She gestured to all the chairs and tables. "I bought some chairs from the town down the road, but Byron made the tables for me."

"You know, I think he's got a plethora of jobs to choose from," PJ said with a small laugh. "Baker, woodworker, fisherman."

"Fisherman?"

"Never mind," PJ said. "Thank you for the refund. If you need help with the dishes or tidying up afterward—or with dinner—I'm happy to help."

PJ, who'd never seen a potato he couldn't peel, spent the next hour in the kitchen with Wendy. She was actually quite nice, though still a bit rough around the edges. PJ asked about her late husband, and where she'd grown up, and what they'd done before the war. She was eager to share all of it, especially to talk about her husband, who'd been the love of her life.

"There was something… I don't know. It felt like he'd somehow arranged for the inn to need a keeper," she said, stirring the large pot of beef stew atop the oven. "It gave me purpose, allowed me to come out of the sadness of losing him. I like to cook, and I don't mind meeting new people, either."

"Did you really..." PJ cleared his throat. "Turn away those magical folk just because they were magical?"

"Bah." She shook her head. "That's Mary meddling in things again. I don't personally have anything against magical folk—as long as they aren't shooting butterflies at my face." She paused, looking at him. "I take it you haven't figured that out yet?"

PJ slowed his peeling. "I think I have. But I don't know how I can fix it."

"Just tell them to stop, eh?" Wendy said. "Or figure out who stirred up the hornet's nest. And get *that* person to stop doing it."

"I think the queen stirred it up, to be honest," PJ said, turning back to the potato to inspect it for any remaining peel. "Whoever it is harbors a lot of anger. I don't know how you can mend those kinds of wounds. Or if that's even possible."

"So we're just going to have to deal with being attacked by flocks of butterflies forever?" Wendy said. "I don't even know what I did to them. They can't hold a grudge against me for just living here. The inn was already built when I arrived. I didn't tear down the Pearlwinds' store."

PJ realized he might've let slip too much. "Well, we went to the property and found it abandoned. So if they're back, they aren't showing themselves to us.

The property, though… Let's just say it wasn't happy to have us wandering around."

"Is that why you showed up covered in mud?"

PJ nodded. "Not our finest hour. Though we've been through worse."

"Hm." She took the potato from him to chop and add to the large stock pot. "Well. Glad to know no one's there, at least. But I'm sure you'll find some way to stop it. That's what you do, right? For Dag Flanigan? You solve magical problems."

"Yeah," PJ said, not wanting to tell her they'd already made up their minds to leave. "That's what we do."

~

When the meal was ready, PJ helped Wendy get everything out to the front room. The only thing missing, in his estimation, was a few loaves of rosemary bread, but Wendy didn't seem to be a baker, and PJ wasn't about to ask the Wersts if they had any to spare. Once the food was out, Wendy waved him away to eat.

"You've done more than enough to pay for your night," she said as Ygritte queued up to get food. "Please, just eat and enjoy the evening."

PJ was more than happy to do that, joining the table with Ygritte, Orville and his husband Toby, and a couple of other farmers. The empty seat next to PJ was eventually filled by Grant, who seemed a little confused by the abrupt change in energy in the room. Unsurprisingly, he'd been upstairs sleeping while PJ had been making inroads with Wendy.

"I'll tell you later," PJ said under his breath.

"But we are leaving tomorrow, right?" Grant replied.

"Leaving?" Ygritte said with a gasp. "But you haven't found the culprit!"

"Yeah, but it doesn't seem anyone around here wants us to be successful," Grant said before shoveling a spoonful of potatoes into his mouth. "Espefially no' tha' ma'or."

"That Mary. She's the worst." Ygritte scowled. "If you ask me, we should have another election and see about kicking *her* out of office. Not as if she's done much to help anyone around here. Or deal with our riffraff situation."

"Or the butterflies," PJ said, remembering what Wendy had said about Mary being in over her head.

"So did those cookies work?" Ygritte asked with a wag of her eyebrows.

"Yeah, and are there any left?" Orville said.

"No, they didn't work," Grant said. "And no, there aren't any left. The recipient dumped them on the ground because she found out the chocolate came from the Wersts."

Ygritte made a noise, sharing a look with Orville as her eyes lit up. "I *told* you they were for the

Pearlwinds!"

"It's not the…" PJ gave Grant a "*please stop talking*" look, but his friend just shrugged.

"We're leaving. Who cares? If she's so mad she's sending butterflies to attack people, then what does it matter if the town knows she's there?" Grant said. "She called herself Petunia Pearlwind. No clue if that's her real name. Maybe she's a long-lost cousin. Said she was married to one of the witches there."

"So there *are* witches still alive over there?"

The energy at the table shifted as every head turned around to find Carl standing behind them.

"You must've misheard us," Orville said, his husband moving closer to him, as if to show a united front. "You three mind your own business."

"It is our business, when it comes to this butterfly stuff," Carl said, his gaze sliding to PJ. "Considering these newcomers haven't lifted a finger to help."

"We're working on it," PJ said before Grant could respond. "And we don't need your help."

"I don't think you understand, *boy*." He spat the word as if PJ were a petulant child. "Me and my friends here, we used to be real good at weeding out magical folk. Whole towns, sometimes. And back at my house, I still have all the fun little iron weapons that can do real damage." His eyes glinted maliciously. "So I'll start with the axe. And see where it goes from there."

"Don't you *dare*," Ygritte said, rising from the table. "Those Pearlwinds have been through enough."

"Sounds like it's not even the Pearlwinds living there anymore," Carl continued, looking down at Grant, who no longer seemed quite as nonchalant as he had before. "Sounds like it's some stranger living under the Pearlwind name. Either way, we don't like magical folks in our town. And we'll be *sure* to send a message that their presence is unwelcome—in one way or another."

"Until such time that we are *no longer* employed by the mayor," Grant said, sounding much more confident than PJ was sure he felt, "we aren't in need of your services."

"Are you telling me what to do?" Carl said, taking another menacing step toward the table. "Because I don't take—"

"I think it's time for you to go," Wendy said, her voice cutting through even Carl's loud tone. "You'll not harass my guests anymore, Carl."

He turned, his very short attention span now focused on Wendy. She kept his gaze, but beneath her sturdy stance was a tremor of fear.

"Clearly, you didn't learn your lesson last time," Carl said. "Because as I was trying to say, I don't take orders anymore. I *give* them."

He nodded to his two henchmen, who walked over to one of the full tables and pushed two men from their seats. The henchmen took the chairs and slammed them hard against the table, shattering them completely and leaving deep gashes on the tabletop. They repeated the process for every chair around the table, until there were none left.

The dragon let out a roar in PJ's mind, but he took steadying breaths to keep from losing control. He wasn't sure of the extent of his own power, and when faced with dangerous soldiers like this in Pigsend, he'd been told to keep his head down and pretend he was normal. Dragon shifters had been decimated under the queen's rule, so he forced himself to stay calm.

Thankfully, when the damage was done, Carl thumbed toward the door. "Let's go. This place reeks of country bumpkins." He flashed a grin at Wendy. "Be sure to clean this up. We'll be back tomorrow." He pointed toward Grant and PJ. "And you two *boys* have until sunset tomorrow to fix this mess. Or I'm going to fix it for you."

Chapter Sixteen

As soon as the door closed, Ygritte rushed over to Wendy, Orville and his husband went to clean the chairs up, and PJ and Grant remained where they were, PJ still trying to tame the dragon in his mind, and Grant watching the clean up with mild interest.

"I suppose I'll have to go back to Timberson to get more chairs," Wendy said. "Ask Byron to stop by in the morning to see about the table. Goodness, he's going to be so upset. He worked so hard on these."

"This just isn't right, Wendy," Ygritte said, patting her on the shoulder. "You shouldn't have to fight off this monster every night, or kowtow to his whims. Someone needs to *do* something about him."

"You're welcome to try," Wendy said, walking to the kitchen and reappearing with a broom to sweep up the mess. "I've already raised it with Mary, and she says until we get something from *His Majesty*, we're on our own out here." She shrugged. "Who's going to arrest him? Quentin? Can't even look Carl in the face."

"We're stronger together," Orville said. "We could gather a coalition and demand he leave."

"And then we'll find our barns on fire and our livestock let out," another farmer said. "I say we just wait for the king's folks. They've been in power a few months now. They should be sending someone to keep the peace any day now."

"And in the meantime, we just let him destroy our property?" Ygritte said with a firm shake of her head. She turned to PJ and Grant. "It'd be nice if that butterfly person would send a swarm to rough *him* up, eh? Then he might be scared enough to leave."

"Yeah, about that," Grant said, turning to PJ— but his eyes bulged. "Whoa there, red eyes," he whispered. "Take a breath, will you?"

PJ started, catching wind of the smoke coming from inside his belly. Perhaps he hadn't tamed the dragon as much as he'd thought.

"We'll be right back," Grant said with a nervous smile.

PJ let Grant drag him up the stairs, but he wasn't finished with the conversation down there, either. Something had to be done, about the butterflies, about Carl, about all of it. And PJ had a feeling he'd be the one to do it. He just hadn't the faintest idea *how*.

Grant closed the door to their room and let out a breath. "Man, what a mess down there, eh? They need to send someone to the king to ask for help. I wonder if it's like this in all the towns. Creeps like Carl taking the law into their own hands." He finally met PJ's gaze. "Are you all right? You aren't about to sprout wings, are you?"

"We need to help them," PJ said, a plume of smoke coming from his lips. He quickly waved it away. "We can't leave, Grant."

"What?" Grant made a face. "We'd be smart to leave tonight, with the way things are going. Did you know that Carl guy had all kinds of anti-magic weaponry?"

"No, but—"

"It's not safe for you to stick around, Peej," Grant said with concern in his gaze. "He's already got it in for us because the mayor hired us to fix the problem. If he finds out what you are…" He shook his head. "The town can fend for itself. We gotta get outta here."

"So we're just going to leave Petunia—"

"That's not her name."

"Whatever her name is. She's a person. You're just going to leave her at that ogre's mercy?" PJ said, his anger roaring back to life again. "Because thanks to you, everyone in town knows someone's there. And I don't think Carl's going to be dissuaded from taking matters into his own hands. Tomorrow at sunset, he said."

"He won't get past those wards," Grant said with a wave of his hand. "I'm sure—"

"Are you? Because I'm not," PJ said. "In fact, I think it's only because he *didn't* know someone was there that he hadn't already taken his iron axes to the forest."

"Well?" Grant said with a wince. "If it solves the problem?"

"It doesn't, though," PJ said, getting to his feet. The dragon was starting to pace in his mind, and if he didn't calm down soon, he *was* going to burn the place down. "What if Petunia's innocent?"

"That's not our problem," Grant said. "We don't live here. We'll probably even forget this place exists after a month. Besides that, Peej, you have a real job to do—and it's not saving small towns from big bullies or random magical attacks. You're supposed to be—"

"I know what I'm supposed to be doing," PJ growled, another plume of smoke rising from his mouth.

"Then let's get on with it," Grant said. "And calm down. Seriously. You're scaring me."

PJ burned with annoyance—both that he saw Grant's logic and resented it. He did need to be getting on with his true task, but leaving now meant not taking responsibility for all the problems they'd caused. Had they not saved Benny, Carl wouldn't know that Petunia was living at the Pearlwind property. He owed it to her to make sure she was safe.

"You go, then," PJ said, his voice low.

"What?"

"Leave in the morning." PJ stomped toward the window. His eyes glowed in the reflection. "If you're so smart about what to do. Go off and find a dragon shifter and see what happens."

"Peej, this isn't my—"

"Yeah, I thought so," PJ replied, watching sparks of fire come out of his mouth in the window. "You're just going to do what you always do. Give up at the first hard moment."

Grant scoffed. "What's that supposed to mean?"

"Exactly what I said," PJ said, turning back around to face his friend. "It was the same in

Pigsend. In Sheepsburg. With every job you've ever had. You just give it a half-hearted try and, when things don't work out, you wash your hands of it, ignoring the consequences."

Grant made a strangled noise.

"I wanted to stay in university," PJ said, finally letting out all the anger he'd been holding in. "I wanted to make something of myself, not just be a farrier or a farmhand or whatever else I was doomed to do if I stayed in Pigsend. And I thought, sure, I can babysit Grant. How hard can it be?" He shook his head. "I should've known better. My dreams depended on you making just a *little* bit of effort. But no. You couldn't even do that."

"I tried my hardest—" Grant said, his voice small.

"You tried just as much as you thought you needed to skirt by," PJ said. "That's how it always is with you. This town, these people, they need help. You can't tell me you didn't feel something listening to them. They don't have options. No one is coming to save them."

"Then why didn't you do anything about it?" Grant asked.

"What?"

"When Carl was in the dining room, threatening Petunia and destroying Wendy's furniture, why didn't you step up?" Grant asked, throwing his hands in the air. "Let the dragon out. Show him what you really are. How powerful and magic and *noble* and *brave*."

"Because I don't know what'll happen if I do," PJ said through gritted teeth.

"Exactly," Grant said, softening a little. "Look, you're right. I'm not great at a lot of things. But I've always looked out for you—and that's what I'm doing now." He let out a breath. "Peej, you're about to march headfirst into trouble I'm not sure I can talk my way out of, you know? I could understand it if it was for Pigsend, for people who love us. But this is a town full of strangers. Strangers who—for the most part—don't want us involved." He tilted his head. "These people aren't worth you getting hurt."

"Yes, they are," PJ said, walking toward the door, his pulse beating in his ears. "I'm going for a walk. Don't wait up."

Nobody in the dining room downstairs said a word to PJ—or if they did, he didn't hear it. Blood pounded in his ears as he stormed away from the inn, the square, and down the road toward the forest. He hadn't meant to erupt at Grant like that, but he was getting tired of the naysaying.

PJ was the one tasked to find more shifters.

PJ was the one sticking his neck out, hiding who

he really was.

PJ was the one making inroads in the town—and it had come back tenfold. Ygritte had convinced Wendy to stop treating them like the enemy, they had a free place to sleep, and…

…and PJ was no closer to solving any of the problems he'd come here to solve.

He slowed his pace, exhaling deeply. As his anger ebbed away, shame replaced the fury, and he felt awful for what he'd said to his best friend. Knowing Grant, he'd probably shrug it off and act like nothing had happened. But PJ had cut him deep, the way only best friends could. The way Grant could hurt him, if he had a mind to.

"I'm not great at a lot of things. But I've always looked out for you—and that's what I'm doing now."

Grant *had* always looked out for PJ. When they'd gotten in trouble, Grant had never once cast the blame on PJ or Valta or anyone else. He'd simply twisted the truth to get them *all* out of it—or they'd all gone down together. And when Grant had every reason to abandon PJ during his first shift, he hadn't. In fact, he'd protected PJ, going so far as to cause a massive diversion when Dag Flanigan got too close to the truth.

But nothing PJ had said about Grant was false, either. It drove PJ absolutely batty at times, the way Grant would shirk responsibilities whenever it got too difficult—and usually act like he was doing the right thing.

But Grant was *also* right that PJ was acting impulsively, wanting to stick it out in Gilramore even when all the odds were stacked against them. There could be a dragon shifter just down the road, sprouting wings and taking flight, and PJ was spending all his time in this town, dealing with butterflies.

"Where are you going?" The sound of a small voice snapped PJ from his thoughts. He looked up into the nearby tree, where Benny was sitting in the branches.

"What are you doing up there?" PJ asked.

"My mom's working late, and my dad had to run an errand," he replied, climbing down. "My grandma told me I was being too loud."

"So naturally, you decided to climb a tree?" PJ asked with a quirked brow.

"I'm still on our land," he said, defensively. "See? The barn's right over there."

PJ squinted into the distance and spotted the red barn. He really hadn't been watching where he was going.

"You looked mad," Benny said. "Are you mad?"

"A little," PJ said. "More frustrated."

"Why?"

"Because nobody wants to tell me anything," PJ

said, eyeing him. "Did you get those cookies?"

"Cookies?" Benny's eyes widened. "What cookies?"

PJ supposed Ygritte had kept the lot for herself, then. "Never mind. You should go home before your folks get back. I don't want your mom madder at me than she already is."

He made a noise. "Why haven't you come back for dinner? Are you really a troublemaker, like my mom says?"

"Depends on who you ask, I suppose," PJ said, looking back the way he'd come. "Your dad told me those butterflies attacked you when you fell into the water."

"I mean, I saw 'em. But I didn't think they were…" He made a face. "My dad was trying to get them away from his face, and he accidentally bumped me. I didn't think they were *attacking* him, at least not like they did our neighbor. Dad said they were gone as soon as I fell in. He wasn't all scratched up the way Quentin or Mr. Gibbons were, in any case."

PJ made a noise. That was a good point, though he had no clue what it meant.

"Thanks for telling me," PJ said, ruffling his hair. "Don't worry. I'm going to find out who's hurting people. And why."

Benny smiled. "I'm not worried. You're cool. I

especially liked it when your eyes glowed red just now."

"Just a trick of the light," PJ said with a laugh. "Now get home."

PJ stood on the fence line and made sure Benny made it all the way to his front porch. Despite the boy's parents' clear distrust, PJ had grown a little fond of the family. Benny, especially, seemed to have a good heart, which usually came from having good parents. He wished there was a way he could get Abigail to let down her guard.

"Perhaps if I stop the attacks," PJ mused.

He made another sweep of Burt Gibbons's property, just to make sure he hadn't missed anything and to water the flowers again. It was a small act of kindness, and no one had painted the ornery registrar out to be anything more than a meanie, but flowers didn't care where they were planted, and they looked thirsty. He knelt and inspected their buds, checking for the millionth time for something magical about them.

"What am I missing?" he muttered to himself. "What did you do to start these attacks?"

He walked the length of the property, searching for anything out of the ordinary as he turned the attacks over in his mind repeatedly. Byron and Mr. Gibbons were neighbors, and their property was close to the Pearlwinds. But Wendy and Quentin were farther away. It could very well have been a vendetta against in the town, but why now? What had changed that had caused the attacks to begin in the first place?

And what did it mean that no one had been seriously hurt, only scratched up?

Too many questions. Not enough answers. And PJ's head was starting to hurt.

He pulled his amulet from under his shirt to inspect it. The letter he'd written the grannies hadn't left Wendy's desk yet, but he really wanted to talk with them. Talk with someone who was smarter about these things than he was. But Petunia wasn't going to talk with him, even if she knew more than she was letting on. Grant would be no help. And the people of Gilramore were as much in the dark as he was.

I here.

"Well, where have you been?" PJ said, not caring if anyone came upon him talking to himself.

Here. Observe.

"Great. Observe." He should probably have a little more tact for the monster living in his head, but after the day he'd had, he was still on edge. "Well? What do you think after all this observation?"

Stop bully.

Carl's face flashed in PJ's mind. "I don't disagree, but is he the most pressing matter? And what should we do about it?"

Butterflies.

PJ blew air between his lips. "You're not making

sense. But I'm talking to myself, and there's a really good chance I've just made you up in my mind."

The dragon seemed similarly flustered.

"Obviously, Carl is a concern," PJ said, starting to walk again. He thought better when he was moving. "But so is the mystery attacker. And nobody wants to tell me the truth."

I see truth.

"Yeah?" That could've come in handy earlier. "How."

Quiet. Me see.

PJ had no clue what that meant but gave in to the feeling of letting go. The dragon unfurled in his mind, taking his senses in a way it hadn't before. The world swam, so PJ closed his eyes to keep from swooning. But as soon as his lids shut, the dragon opened his own, seeing a much different world.

"Whoa."

The colors of the forest were now completely inverted. What had been green was now purple, what had been empty was now full. He could see farther and clearer than he'd ever seen before, and details he'd missed were now obvious. To his left, a small winged creature flitted from tree to tree near a clearing. To his right, a family of owls slept in a hollowed-out tree. Bunnies, squirrels, and other creatures scurried between the tree roots. He could even sense an ant pile, with its inhabitants on the move, just to the left of his foot.

Find butterflies.

The dragon moved PJ's feet deeper into the forest, crunching over the thick thorns and tangles of vines that released green, earthy scents. If not for the dragon's steady control of his mind, he would've been overwhelmed by his heightened senses, but the dragon seemed intent on finding something—the way it had when PJ had saved Benny.

PJ spotted a deep pool of silvery liquid up ahead. "What's that?"

Magic.

"Just in a pool like that?" PJ asked.

Humans no see.

But PJ certainly saw it, especially as the dragon bent his knees to kneel before it. He touched the shimmering surface which was as light as air and as powerful as…well, himself.

"Where did it come from?" PJ asked.

Land.

PJ nodded. Pigsend had a magical river running beneath it, but he'd always pictured an underground river of water in his mind. Not this silvery, powerful, harnessable magic that was just sitting in a pool near the queen's stronghold. Did the townsfolk even know it was here? He was pretty far off the road now, and he doubted anyone would *want* to walk through all this muck.

"Is this what we're looking for?" PJ asked.

No. Butterflies.

PJ was back on his feet in an instant, trudging faster this time. He really, *really* hoped the dragon had a good sense of direction, because PJ had no clue where they were in relation to Gilramore. As he loudly crunched through the forest, he scared off more nonmagical creatures.

"If we're trying to sneak up on something," PJ said, "we should, perhaps, be a little quieter."

You quiet. I search.

An invisible hand yanked PJ in another direction, and he stumbled as he almost lost his balance. But soon enough, he came upon a large tree bathed in a small patch of the dwindling sunlight that had made its way through the canopy above. It almost looked out of place, with large, golden broad leaves and—

Wait, not leaves.

"There they are," PJ breathed, approaching as quietly as possible.

The butterflies covered the tree, which had no leaves at all, he realized. They certainly looked like normal bugs now, opening and closing their wings slowly as they rested on the tree. They didn't seem concerned by PJ's approach, even when he got close enough to see their small antennae and legs clinging to the branches.

No magic.

PJ nodded. "Then someone's making them attack. Casting a spell."

Witch.

"I don't know where—"

But PJ's feet moved unbidden as the dragon sensed the world in front of him, but also the world behind and ahead of him. He'd walked a long way, but he'd gone mostly parallel to the road, so it wasn't that hard to get back on it and take the easier route toward the Pearlwind property. He was grateful no one else was traveling, because he probably looked strange, stumbling around, talking to himself, presumably with glowing red eyes.

The Pearlwinds' property was much easier to find through the dragon's senses, as the wards were so glaringly obvious. Getting through them would still be difficult, though, as the magical threads seemed tightly woven together with the vines, branches, and bushes like a thick sweater.

"Shall we?" PJ asked.

Wait.

The magical vision shifted once more, and PJ realized he could see *through* the wards now. But the vision before him was much different than the one in his mind.

The house was no longer falling apart. Now, it was a sturdy, well-constructed dwelling with an *intact* thatched roof and a stone chimney that emitted purple smoke. Surrounding the home were rows and rows of vibrant green gardens, spilling over the bounds of their raised beds and climbing up trellises. There were pops of reds and purples from berries, large green cucumbers, and bright orange pumpkins and other squashes. A massive apple tree sat just feet from that garden and was laden with more fruit than anything PJ had seen on Ygritte or Orville's farms.

But most surprising was the middle-aged woman humming to herself as she carried a large wicker basket, plucking the bounty from the plants with ease as she walked without a cane. Her hair was brown with only flecks of gray, and her skin was without a single wrinkle. She reached into the basket, pulled out one of the cookies PJ had brought her, and took a hearty bite. She sighed happily before plucking a bunch of blackberries. Then, earning another gasp of horror from PJ, she twisted her fingers around the plucked blackberry vines, and the plant grew, sprouting five more bright white flowers that would eventually turn into fruit.

As if summoned, a single golden butterfly came fluttering over to land on her finger.

PJ's eyes snapped open, the world now back to green and blues instead of the inverted colors. His anger roared back to life. "That lying little… "

Calm. Get truth first.

PJ clicked his tongue, debating whether to march through the wards and the vines to harangue whoever was really living in the house. It was clear they'd been lying about, well, *everything*. From the state of their house to the fact that they *had* magic. Their name was the least of PJ's worries, though he had a hunch this was probably Venalda, the plant-growing sister.

"Maybe I should let Carl go after her," PJ said, looking around. "Since she's so keen on—"

Good reason.

"Yeah, he does have a good reason—"

She lie good reason.

The words settled in PJ's mind and, once again, he hated the logic. Of course Venalda would lie to him. She was a magical creature who'd been hiding in plain sight all these years. The townsfolk hadn't even known she was there, but when a creature like PJ waltzed into her property, she had to give him something. Saying she wasn't magical, acting like she was in a house that was falling apart… It was a good cover story.

"But why the chocolate chip cookies?" PJ muttered. That seemed so random.

The dragon exhaled, and it sounded like a laugh.

"So you think she wanted me to go on a wild goose chase so I'd give up and not come back?"

Yes.

"Well, that's just taking advantage of my good nature," PJ said, his cheeks burning.

Why hadn't he questioned it at all? He'd been so focused on helping, on soothing her wounds, that he hadn't seen how ridiculous the request was. And believing her when she said the land was sentient. No wonder she'd been able to play him so readily.

Fooled us both.

PJ frowned. "You, too, hm? So you aren't all-knowing and all-powerful?"

You learn. I learn.

That was disappointing. PJ gave the forest one more look before turning back to walk to Gilramore. "I was hoping you had some deep, ancestral connection to the grannies, or some kind of communal knowledge we could call on."

I know magic. I learn world.

PJ wasn't exactly sure what difference was between them, but at least he knew the dragon had a little more knowledge than he did. "So will you teach me magic?"

Me magic. You world.

PJ chuckled. "Yeah, but—"

Dragon fire consume you. Humans not made for dragon. Me magic. You world. Amulet bridge.

PJ pulled his amulet from beneath his shirt, a chill running through his body. His first and only shift had been terrifying, like something dark and evil wanting to claw out of his skin. He'd done it in the safety of the mountain, with the grannies nearby. But even his own parents had been told to wait in a town at the foot of the mountain, for their own safety. It was, perhaps, a good thing PJ hadn't ever taken off his amulet.

No scare. I control. You fix bully. You find real butterfly. We make town better.

PJ smirked, some of the fear disappearing with the confidence of the dragon's voice. "Let's get back to town, smooth things over with Grant, and get everything out in the open. Then we'll figure out what to do with Carl and this lying witch."

~

By the time PJ arrived at the inn, his pulse had returned to normal, and he hoped his eyes had, too. He'd been grateful none of the townsfolk had seen him as a full dragon (or as full as he wanted to get), but he still felt the smoldering of anger in his mind. He felt absolutely foolish taking what Petunia had said at face-value, and even more foolish for wasting a full day trying to appease her when it was clear she was just trying to get him to leave her alone. His first clue should've been when Ygritte had said there was no bakery, but no. He'd just plowed onward, ignoring what should've been a clear sign that he was being had.

Lesson learned. It wouldn't be the last time someone took advantage of his kindness, but he hoped he'd get better at spotting the difference.

He lingered at the front door of the inn for just a moment, taking one final, calming breath, then opened it. The farmers, along with Mary and Quentin, were still in the dining room, though the mess had been cleared up. PJ hadn't seen Quentin before Carl and his bullies had come inside; perhaps the de facto sheriff had been hiding until the ruffians left.

Mary was talking with Wendy and met PJ's gaze when he walked inside. She quickly finished her conversation and walked up to PJ, looking a little too upbeat for someone whose town was still under attack from butterflies and ogres.

"I need to talk with you," she said. "It seems there was a bit of excitement in the inn tonight."

"Yeah, would be great if the mayor would do something about it," PJ drawled, crossing his arms and feeling the dragon come to the surface again. Perhaps not quite as level-headed as he'd hoped, but he'd grown disillusioned with the mayor at this point.

Mary's eyes flashed. "Well, in that vein, I have good news. Gilramore's no longer in need of your services."

"We got that message already," PJ said with a

quirked brow. "When you told the townsfolk to treat us like pariahs and the innkeeper to overcharge us."

She cleared her throat. "What I mean," she smiled sweetly, "is that I've discovered the problem. And I've fixed it. There will be no more butterfly attacks."

"How did you—?" PJ asked with narrowed eyes.

"I have my ways," she said with a dismissive wave of her hand. "After some investigating of my own, of course. I'm not too busy to solve the problems of my own town." She laughed, and PJ winced at how fake it was. "In any case, there's no need for you to stay another day."

"Mm."

She shifted. "I mean, of course we *do* appreciate all the work you put in. It really was nice of you to stay and help, but... Well, as I said, it's all fixed now. No more need for your services." She pulled out a small bag and handed it to him, coins clinking loudly. "Here's a payment for your effort."

PJ stared at it, warning bells going off in his mind. There was absolutely no way the mayor had dealt with the problem, and while they'd discussed a small fee, the weight of the gold in his hand felt more like a bribe to leave than payment for a job half-finished. But why?

"I, erm, tried to give it to your friend, but he

wouldn't take it," Mary said. "So I hope you'll accept it and be on your way. With our thanks, of course."

PJ turned to Grant, who was watching their interaction with a stony expression, and a burst of affection blossomed in his chest. He pushed the bag back into Mary's hands.

"Our job isn't finished," PJ said. "And as a matter of fact, I think you and I need to have a discussion about the witches living down the road from your house."

"W-witches?" She gave a laugh that seemed even more nervous than before. "You must be mistaken. There's no one living at that house. You told me yourself it was empty."

PJ eyed her, sensing something underneath her too-bright personality. "I was mistaken. There's clearly someone living there. Someone with—"

"Well, I'll be sure to, erm, send Quentin to check it out," she said, cutting him off. "We've got it handled from here on out. We're quite adept at dealing with that sort of folk, if you recall."

"Quentin didn't deal with those butterflies very well," PJ said.

"The butterflies are no longer a problem."

He crossed his arms over his chest, watching her intently. First the very obvious lie about handling the butterflies then the bribe to leave town. Now she was acting like the very mention of *magic* would stir the townsfolk up into a frenzy.

"There are no witches living in or around this town," Mary said to his silence. "I can promise you that. Now." She cleared her throat. "Do be sure to check out early in the morning. I'll send along Quentin to ensure you make it out of town all right."

PJ wanted to argue, but Mary made an excuse about needing to get back to the office to sort some things out, leaving Quentin behind to give him a stern look.

"I'll be by at sunup," he said as if PJ hadn't saved him from butterflies days before. "Don't make this difficult."

"My friend doesn't get up until at least nine, so you'll be waiting a while," PJ said. "And we're not leaving until we find the culprit. I don't care what your mayor says."

"But—"

"You are *welcome* to try to extract us," PJ said, gazing coolly at the soldier. "But you'll have as much success as you do keeping Carl under control."

PJ didn't bother waiting to see his reaction, turning and crossing the room with purpose to sidle up next to Grant, who was talking to Orville in low tones. Orville gave PJ a brief smile then excused himself, saying it was late and he and the husband needed to get home.

Now alone, Grant watched PJ nervously, but PJ cleared his throat. "Sorry about earlier."

"I forgot about it already," Grant said, looking toward the dining room as if avoiding the mushy feelings. "It seems we've been asked to leave town by the mayor."

"Mm." PJ rocked on his heels. "I don't feel quite ready to leave."

"Me neither." He smirked. "Especially as the mayor wants us to go. Seems like she's up to something. Maybe she's sending the butterflies. Wants to shore up her support before the election."

"Is there an election soon?" PJ asked.

"Well, no, not that I've heard, but you know these politicians. They always think ahead." He tapped his forehead. "What better way to solidify her spot than to scare the residents into submission then magically solve it?"

"That's a good theory," PJ said, trying to keep a straight face. "But I found something I think you might find interesting." He glanced around. "C'mon. Let's discuss it upstairs."

CHAPTER EIGHTEEN

"I'm shocked."

Grant wasn't, based on the drawl of his voice, but let PJ tell him about what he'd seen through his dragon's eyes anyway, from finding the butterflies at rest to seeing the Pearlwind witch cast magic on her plants to the house that wasn't falling apart at all—and most importantly, that the witch was controlling the butterflies.

"So what do you think it means?" Grant asked.

"I think it means we march in there, tell her we see right through her magic—"

Glamour.

"Glamour, I mean," PJ corrected, silently

thanking the dragon. "And that she'd better start telling us what's going on, else we'll let Carl have at her."

"I thought she was an innocent old woman, and it wasn't fair—"

"That was before I realized she'd tricked me," PJ said.

"Oh, sweet Peej…" Grant rose and patted PJ on the shoulder. "I coulda told you she'd tricked you. In fact, I'm pretty sure I *did*—"

"Water under the bridge," PJ said with a smile as he considered his friend. "Mary said you declined the big sack of gold."

"The bribe to leave town?" Grant said. "I can be bought, of course, but you have to at least act like it's not a bribe. Otherwise, I'm made to feel like I'm an unsavory character who leaves town at the drop of a hat. And only a horrible person would say something like that to me."

PJ let out a sigh, deflating. "I'm sorry for what I said. I got a little too—"

"Dragon-y?" Grant chuckled. "Goodness, I thought I was about to get my eyebrows singed off. Not like you to fly off the handle like that, you know?"

"Well, I'm frustrated," PJ said.

"Join the club." Grant laughed, but there was something underneath it. He rubbed the back of his head. "You weren't wrong, though. I do quit things too easily. I don't know why. I just feel like..." He looked at his shoes as they tapped on the floor. "I feel like if I don't try, I know I *could* do it, if I *wanted* to. But if I try and..."

"Fail?" PJ offered.

"Then I know I'm a failure," Grant finished, still not meeting PJ's gaze. "And I'm not really sure I want to know that about myself."

"You're not a failure, no more than I'm a rube for falling for that witch's trick," PJ said. "We make mistakes, but we pick each other up afterward. That's why we're a good team."

"Yeah, but we're missing a crucial element in Valta," Grant said with a shake of his head. "She never let us come to blows. Always had a knack for cooling us off before we got too into it." He squinted toward the window. "What are the odds her parents changed their minds about her joining us?"

"Slim to none," PJ said. "But we should drop her a letter when this is all over. Goodness knows she probably needs some entertainment."

"Yeah, well, we gotta figure out what's happening before we can regale her with the story," Grant said, slapping his knees. "What's our next step, boss? Or should I be talking to the dragon?" His eyes glinted. "And what *exactly* is going on with that, anyway?"

PJ shrugged. "He's there. He's been chattier lately. He says I'm supposed to navigate this world, and he'll handle the dragon magic when necessary."

"Is he the one providing the gold?" Grant asked.

Not me. From hoard. A vision of a giant cave with hills and hills of gold and silver coins came into PJ's mind.

"We were right, it's from a large, erm…stash." PJ decided he would *never* let Grant anywhere near that cave. His friend might die from happiness. "He doesn't really know much about the real world. I think he was asleep this whole time. With the old amulet."

"Huh." Grant tilted his head.

"In any case, he thinks we should deal with Carl *and* the butterflies. Which means we need to confront the Pearlwind woman and figure out who she really is and why she's attacking the town."

"Sounds good," Grant said with a yawn. "But I'm exhausted. All this talking and fighting and whatnot takes a toll on a man, you know?"

"You said it," PJ said, sinking down onto his bed and taking off his boots, which were still covered in mud from the forest.

"So what's his name?"

"Who?"

"The dragon."

"He doesn't have a name, I don't think," PJ said.

The dragon made a noise that sounded like a cross between a growl and the bellowing war cry of a thousand soldiers. PJ winced as it rang between his ears.

My name.

"I don't think he has a pronounceable name," PJ corrected, clearing his throat. "But maybe we can call him…"

"How about Tim?" Grant said. "That way we can refer to him in polite company without, erm, raising too many eyebrows."

PJ laughed. "Sure, why not? We can just call him Tim."

~

Surprisingly, Grant was up and ready at a reasonable hour, and when he and PJ came down the stairs, Wendy was waiting, giving them an appraising look.

"Are you checking out today?" she asked. "Haven't seen Quentin yet, but I hear he's coming to escort you out of town."

"We do hope to be getting on our way today," PJ said. "But first, we've got to find some answers."

She grinned, closing her registration book. "Good. I don't believe for a second Mary just *happened* to solve the problem without telling any of us how or who did it or why. I'm sure she's just hoping the problem stops so things return to normal."

PJ nodded, sensing there was much more to Mary than met the eye. But the questions about her would have to go on the back burner. "If Quentin comes by—"

"I'll be sure to let him know you've already left," she said with a knowing wink. "Good luck. And, erm…" She thumbed toward the kitchen. "You might want to go out the back door anyway. I'm not ready for you to leave, but I'm not sure about the rest of the folks around here. A lot of 'em still feel loyal to Mary, and they'd absolutely detain you if they thought she wanted them to."

"Thanks," PJ said.

The duo snuck out through the kitchen, with Grant snatching the two apples left on the table on his way out. "What?" he said, munching on the first. "It's clear those were for us."

They kept a brisk pace, taking a roundabout way through the town, along the back edge of the Gibbons's and Wersts' property, until they were finally on the road leading to the forest. PJ wasn't saying much, gathering the questions in his mind that he planned to lob at the woman, and trying to keep his anger in check. He'd woken up in a slightly better mood, but the more he thought about how she'd taken advantage of his kindness to hide her own guilt, the more it roared between his ears.

He walked up to the thick wall of vines and magic, though he couldn't see the latter with his human eyes, and cleared his throat.

"Open the wards and let us through."

The vines shuddered and tightened their hold, and the magic grew stronger, pushing back against PJ even though he still stood on the road. PJ held his ground, letting a puff of smoke come from his nostrils as he stared down the green foliage.

"I'm coming in peace," he called again, pulling at the leaves that were in arm's reach. "But if you don't open these wards, I'm going to let myself in, and I'm not going to be nice about it. So please, let us in so we can talk about why you're attacking Gilramore."

The vine he poked reached out and slapped his hand.

"Fine," PJ said, wringing his hand and giving Grant a sideways look. "You asked for it."

He let the dragon take over, the red eyes opening behind his own. He opened his mouth, releasing a powerful stream of...

Fire.

PJ was breathing fire.

It consumed the plants, burning them to a crisp and leaving a blackened tunnel that started inches from PJ's boots and ended right where the Pearlwind house stood.

"I'm not sure I meant to do that," PJ said, a little nervously.

Grant, who'd taken several steps back, cleared his throat as if PJ breathing fire were an everyday occurrence. "Well, you did give her a warning. She has no one to blame but herself." He pointed to the plants, which were starting to reknit themselves in the ashes of their brethren. "But we should probably get inside if we don't want to have to do that again."

The boys scrambled through the hole they'd made, fighting off a few vines here and there, before emerging on the other side. The home was once again under the glamour, looking like a dilapidated shack that could barely stand up. But PJ was no longer fooled, seeing the shimmering magic lying atop the roof and walls. Though he couldn't quite see under it, he knew what was really there.

"Reveal yourself," PJ bellowed, some of the dragon's voice mingling with his own. "I know who and what you are. It's no use hiding from me."

"As if I could hide from you!" Venalda appeared, still wearing her Petunia glamour, holding her cane and glaring at PJ and Grant. "You barge in here, burning down my plants. You could've set my home on fire, you fool! And now you've left me open to attack from those monsters down the road."

"He did ask you nicely," Grant said. "And the plants are clearly fine."

PJ glanced behind them, where the vines had reconstructed their thick web already. Besides a few black marks, it was impossible to tell there'd been any kind of hole whatsoever.

"I have nothing to tell you," she said. "I'm not doing anything in Gilramore."

"I saw you with a golden butterfly," PJ said. "It landed on your finger. And there's a whole mess of them not five minutes from your property."

"I don't have any magic," she said, though it sounded less confident than it had before. "I'm ordinary—"

"Peej, show the lady what you can do," Grant said. "Again."

PJ stepped forward and let the dragon come to the surface. Smoke emitted from his mouth, and his eyes burned as he faced the woman.

She took a step back, swallowing nervously. "W-what are you?"

"I don't think you want to find out," PJ said, the dragon making his voice lower. "So how about the truth?"

She licked her lips, looking around nervously for a moment, then exhaled. The magic slid away from the house, the garden, even the woman herself, revealing the younger face and straighter body PJ had seen in his earlier vision. The fire in her eyes, though, hadn't abated, and she took three steps toward him.

"Here's the truth," she said, her voice even higher and younger. "I'm not attacking the town. I would never attack the town, even if some of those monsters deserve it. But the risk of discovery is way too high."

"Is that why you gave me the fake story about Petunia?" PJ asked.

"I was hoping you'd just believe me when I said I didn't have magic," she said. "If I told you who I really was, I knew you'd have more questions."

"What about the butterfly I saw?" PJ said.

"There are golden butterflies all over this forest," she said impatiently. "They like my property because there are flowers everywhere. I'm not sure what you saw or when, but they do come and go. They're not... The ones that come here are just normal bugs."

"Is the land riling them up?" PJ asked, the dragon fading away with his anger. "Maybe doing it without you knowing?"

She shook her head. "Everything on this property is under my guidance. It's not me. Whatever's happening..." She shrugged. "I truly have no idea. Maybe some other magical creature returned and wants to wreak havoc. But I didn't lie to you about leaving the property. I haven't set foot in Gilramore these past six years—and I don't intend to any time soon." She gestured to the garden behind her. "I do really have everything I could ever need here."

She speak truth.

"Except chocolate chip cookies," PJ said, still annoyed. "Which you threw on the ground. Then ate anyway."

"I mean…" She laughed nervously. "It's been six years since I've had anything I didn't grow myself. And a little dirt never bothered me."

"How'd you avoid the queen all these years?" Grant asked. "Especially considering a huge contingent of soldiers was right next door."

"That's not important," she said quickly, her cheeks turning red. "What's important is that you two stop harassing me. I've shown you my true form. I'm sorry for the lies. But I swear, on my property and my plants and my potions, that I'm *not* attacking people in Gilramore."

"What about your siblings?" Grant asked, earning a nod from PJ. "Are they back? Could they be behind it?"

She licked her lips, looking lost for a moment. "The last I heard from them, they were hiding out in an underground haven for magical creatures," she said. "They begged me to come with them, but I couldn't fathom leaving this land behind." She cleared her throat. "I hadn't seen another person until you two barged onto my property."

PJ chewed his lip, glancing at the sky and the position of the sun. How serious had Carl been about his deadline of sundown?

"Who else could it be?" Grant asked. "There's nobody else magical in Gilramore, right?"

"I don't know who's in Gilramore anymore," she said, impatiently. "Because *I haven't left my property.*"

"Then in the woods," PJ said, gesturing to the trees surrounding them. "Have you seen anyone? Sensed any new people?"

"The limits of my powers are my property lines," she said. "If I let my magic wander outside, there's a chance I'd be found out by the queen's people. The Wersts live a stone's throw from here, you know?"

"So you've seen *them*?" Grant asked.

"The family's lived there for generations," she said, almost a little defensively. "The two boys like to wander the woods. I see them on the other side of my wards, which thankfully do their job and deter people from coming too close."

PJ rubbed his forehead. They were back at square one, then. Worse than square one, because he was getting the sense Venalda was telling the truth.

Which meant there was *something else* PJ had

been missing. But what could it be?

"The people who were attacked were Burt Gibbons, Byron Werst, Quentin the soldier, and Wendy the innkeeper," PJ said, talking to himself more than Venalda. "Have you seen any of them out in the woods?"

"I don't know who several of those are, but yes, I see people in the woods all the time," she said. "The Werst boys, as I said, but other people, too."

What that?

PJ felt it, too: an anger—a fury, actually. He tilted his head up toward the sky and saw the butterflies swirling, agitated, as they fluttered toward Gilramore.

Chapter Nineteen

Venalda was kind enough to lower her wards so PJ didn't have to burn his way through them, and the boys ran the short distance back to town, which was completely inundated with swarms of golden butterflies. The attacker seemed to have gathered every insect in the nearby forest—and then some—and launched a full-scale assault on the village. The farmers' stands were all in shambles, the town hall had lost part of its roof, the inn's front door had been torn off its hinges.

The town square was a chaotic mess of people. Unemployed soldiers swung swords and shields to keep the insects away from their faces. Mary ran in circles, trying to dissuade the swarm that had decided to pull every one of her pins out of her hair. Byron had his two boys cowering at his feet as he used a rake to break up the attack. Quentin was hiding behind a bush, but the butterflies had found him, too. Orville and Ygritte had taken large pieces of their farm stands and were using them as weapons, but the butterflies were faster than everyone.

Me fix.

"Yeah, but where to first?" PJ said, looking around wildly.

"Peej, over here!" Grant called, waving him over to where Byron and the boys were hunkered down. PJ ran over and quickly broke the spell, earning a sigh of relief from Byron.

"Get the boys inside the inn," PJ said.

Byron didn't need to be told twice, scooping both kids up and running toward the nearby inn. But inside, there were even *more* butterflies. After having torn down all the queen's colors, they were now picking up Wendy's few remaining chairs and smashing them on the ground.

PJ stood in the doorway and felt for the thread of magic, which was coming from the kitchen. He dashed inside, let out a loud *roar* that snapped the thread, then came back out into the dining room.

"Everyone okay?" PJ asked.

"Peej!" Grant called from outside.

"I'll be back in a moment!"

Next up were the farmers, which proved to be trickier as there were no fewer than three streams of magic to break up, all braided together like a rope. The dragon was growing as frustrated as PJ, but finally—*finally*—he found the original thread and snapped it.

The magic that had surrounded the square evaporated almost instantly, and the butterflies took to the sky, filling it with a golden shimmer as they returned to their home.

PJ exhaled loudly as he came back to himself fully, his mind whirling.

"W-what happened?" Orville said, putting down the makeshift weapon.

"I thought you said you stopped this," Ygritte bellowed at Mary, who was helping Quentin to his feet.

"I thought I did," she said softly, her dark hair plastered to her face and her tunic torn in several places. "I don't know what…" She looked at PJ, shock still evident on her face. "You stopped it?"

He nodded, looking to the sky once more. "I think we need to sit down and have a conversation about what's really going on." He pointed to the inn. "Everyone. *Inside.*"

"Erm, there's nowhere to sit," Wendy said.

PJ let out a breath. "Fine. To the town hall."

PJ wasn't in the mood to entertain arguments, so he was grateful the crowd migrated without complaint. Mary got sidetracked when Abigail arrived carrying young Margo, and they both insisted on checking the crowd for signs of major injury. But everyone just looked bedraggled. Like they'd been attacked by a flock of butterflies.

"So I think we can safely take Venalda off the list, eh?" Grant muttered, walking up beside PJ with a smirk.

"I think so," PJ said with a nod. "I don't think she'd be able to cast that kind of magic and talk to us at the same time."

"What does Tim think?"

"Who's..." PJ snorted. He'd forgotten Grant had renamed his dragon.

Agree.

PJ nodded. "Tim agrees. So who are our suspects?"

"Nobody," Grant said, looking around. "Unless one of these townsfolk has a great, big secret they don't want to share with anyone."

"There's got to be a reason for it. Quentin is understandable—he's magical but worked for the queen. Byron brought the queen's folks here. Wendy's a bit of a stretch, because she only took over the inn after it was built. But I could see someone having a vendetta against her. But attacking the farm stands, too? That seems like…"

"Someone's got another ulterior motive," Grant said with a nod. "But what? Is there anything that connects them?"

PJ shook his head. "The other thing that's interesting is none of the attacks have really caused a lot of harm."

"Benny falling in the river wasn't harm?"

"I don't think they meant for him to fall in," PJ said. "They were attacking Byron, who bumped into Benny. Once that happened, the spell broke immediately."

"Huh." Grant rubbed his chin. "So you're saying that someone has a lot of anger but doesn't want anyone seriously hurt. Just give them a few scratches, destroy some property, and be done with it?"

Odd.

Tim's voice echoed in PJ's head, and he focused on the word and the replay of the latest attack in his mind. There *was* a lot odd about the latest attack— especially as the spell had definitely come from somewhere east of Venalda's property. Even if Carl was successful in getting through the wards, it wouldn't solve the actual problem, because neither the witch nor her land had originated this latest attack.

"The spell was coming from the forest, then," PJ said, after a minute. "Farther east than the Pearlwinds."

"What's there?" Grant asked.

"Not much. A few pools of magic. Lots of trees." He rubbed his forehead. "As much as I don't want to, I think our next move is canvassing the forest, looking for whoever did this."

I help.

And Tim would help.

"It looks like we're all okay," Mary said, approaching the boys with a nervous smile. "Thank you for for whatever you did." She nodded to her brother and nephews. "I don't know what I'd do if anything happened to them."

"I suppose you really didn't do anything to fix the problem?" PJ asked plainly.

She stared at him, shocked. "No, I did. I was… Well, I suppose it didn't work, did it? It doesn't matter now."

"Is there another magical person in Gilramore?" Grant asked.

She shook her head. "There are no magical people in this town. Period, end of story."

"What about just outside?" PJ asked. "In the forest? At the Pearlwind property? Do you consider that part of your town?"

Mary's jaw tightened. "Are you going to speak to the crowd or not?"

PJ glared at her, wishing she'd stop beating around the bush and just tell him what she was hiding. But instead, he walked to the front of the room, where every eye in the room was on him, and wanting answers. But beyond their fury, he found fear. Angst. Worry that no one was safe. And a hope that the young man at the front of the room would save them.

Is this how Bev felt?

"Erm, is everyone all right?" PJ asked. "I know we've suffered some more damage—"

"My inn's destroyed!" Wendy cried.

"My stand is gone. Again!" Orville said, standing up. "I thought you said you'd fixed this, Mary. What gives?"

"Yes, Mary, what gives?" Grant asked, looking over at her.

"Don't blame her," Byron said, standing next to his sister. They resembled each other more than PJ had thought—except Byron was two heads taller. "Someone wants to hurt the people of Gilramore. They've made it painfully obvious. We need to find out who it is."

"It's probably one of those magical folks returning," one of the farmers said. "Wanting to retaliate against the queen."

"What quarrel would they have with me?" Orville retorted. "I'm not a soldier."

"I personally never vowed fealty to the queen," Ygritte said, crossing her arms over her chest. "So they shouldn't have anything to say to *me*."

"It's those registrars!" another farmer called. "Someone wants to get revenge on them! And we're just getting swept up in the mix!"

"Then why aren't they the ones with destroyed property?" Orville shot back.

"Everyone, please," PJ said, holding up his hands. Despite his young voice, the crowd actually listened. "Look, I think the best thing to do is to lay out exactly what happened—in chronological order."

Byron shifted, glancing at his wife nervously.

"And maybe, together, we can come up with a logical explanation." PJ glanced behind him at Grant, who gave him a thumbs-up. "So let's start with the first attack—"

"I didn't do anything," Quentin said. "Was just minding—"

"You weren't the first," PJ said, earning a gasp from the crowd. "The first was Burt Gibbons. Right, Mary?"

She looked annoyed but nodded.

"Why weren't we told?" Orville said with a loud frown.

"What else are you keeping from us, Mary?" Ygritte bellowed.

"The second attack," PJ cut in, "was Byron."

Abigail spun toward her husband. "What? Are you—"

"Fine." He gave PJ a pleading look then let out a sigh. "Benny and I were fishing by the creek. A flock of 'em came around. I…erm… Benny fell in—"

"*What*?" Abigail and Mary said in unison.

"We can, erm, discuss that part later," PJ said. "Byron, was there anything about that day that stood out to you?"

He shook his head. "I'd finished up with Wendy's furniture that morning. Grabbed Benny around lunchtime. Then we went straight to the creek."

Abigail glowered at her husband. "We will *absolutely* discuss this later."

"Quentin?" PJ turned to the soldier. "What about you? Anything strange about the day you were attacked?"

He shifted. "I finished up some chores at the house that morning. But otherwise, nothing."

"What kind of chores?" PJ asked.

"A few of my fence posts were broken," he said.

"Byron, what about your neighbor, Burt?" PJ asked. "Did he mention anything strange about when he was attacked? He wasn't helping you two with Wendy's furniture, was he?"

"You can't be serious," Abigail scoffed. "You think we're all being attacked by butterflies because of Wendy's furniture?"

"We're looking at all angles," Grant said from behind PJ. "And if you have anything to add, please do so. Otherwise, keep your opinions to yourself."

Abigail wilted a little.

"I'd like to say what we're all thinking," Ygritte said, rising and looking around. "And that's the possibility that the Pearlwinds are back in town." She nodded to PJ. "What was all that about the chocolate chips? You said you were bringing them to someone to stop the attacks. What happened with that?"

"That person wasn't involved," PJ said, his cheeks reddening a little. "Erm. That was… A bit of a wild goose chase, I admit."

"Somebody's at the Pearlwind property," Ygritte said. "You said it was some woman calling herself Petunia. So there's a squatter there."

"That's impossible," Mary chimed in. "The Pearlwinds are long gone. Even with the queen out of power—"

"Clearly, someone with magic is in town pretending to be them," Orville said. "And I had no quarrel with the Pearlwinds before, but I'm looking at a second round of rebuilding my farm stand.

Might just pack it in until the spring, to be honest. I can't be rebuilding every few days, you know?"

Some of the other farmers nodded and murmured amongst themselves, nodding.

Mary looked around helplessly then turned to PJ as if he could provide the answers.

"Now might be a good time to come clean," PJ said, low enough so only she could hear. "Tell everyone what's really going on. What you're hiding. Who you spoke to to *fix* the problem—if anyone."

"I don't think you understand," Mary replied, turning to him earnestly. "If I do—"

"I think I've got the solution to our problem." Carl's voice rang out in the town hall, getting everyone's attention. He stood at the front doors, a large double-sided axe resting against his shoulder. He wore an iron breastplate and an iron helmet, as if he were going to war against a magical army.

"What's your solution?" Ygritte asked.

"I'm going to take out that forest," Carl said. "It's clear the Pearlwinds are back. Or someone is. Obviously, our *wonderful* mayor's been hiding something from us. I told her years ago we should clear it all out, expand the town, but she told me to leave it alone." He cracked a smile. "Wonder what's actually there?"

"I was doing you a kindness," Mary said, her

voice steely. "That forest is full of leftover charms and wild magic. You'd be lost in the wards before you got two steps into the mix."

"I'd like to try my luck," he said. "Since it's clear no one else is willing to do what it takes to protect our lovely town."

"I say you let him at it," Orville said. "If it's the Pearlwinds, we can deal with them and make them fix what they broke. But if not, whoever's there needs to be dealt with."

Ygritte looked a little uneasy about it but nodded anyway. "Maybe it's not the Pearlwinds, but their land. Couldn't hurt to have him clear it out a bit. Maybe we'll find those butterflies and get rid of them."

PJ watched the exchange helplessly—that was, until he spotted Grant inching toward the door. They met gazes for a minute, Grant giving PJ the thumbs up, then his friend disappeared out the door.

Mary fidgeted nervously. "Well, if the town is in agreement."

"I, personally, give it my full-throated endorsement," Abigail said, her arms protectively around her boys. "Because this person has little care for the children in this town. They can deal with Carl. And whatever he finds, he can bring back here to face justice."

Mary sighed. "Fine. Carl. Go do your thing. But do be careful. I don't know what you'll find when you get there." She cleared her throat. "And you may want to take some folks with you. Just in case you need some backup, you know?"

"Fine." He nodded toward some of the farmers. "You three. Come with me. We'll get you some armor. Then we'll see what we find in that awful forest."

PJ watched them go nervously. Assuming Venalda would hear Grant through her wards, she'd have time to leave, especially if the goons were gathering equipment and people. Maybe Carl would show up at the house, see the ramshackle house through the glamour, and leave. And if not… Well, a house could be rebuilt.

"We'll convene back here in a few hours, after he's had time to sort through his vendetta," Mary said, looking defeated. "Then we can talk about how to repair the farm stands and the rest of the property that was damaged. In the meantime, I'm going to go make sure no one else was hurt."

Mary walked out of the town hall, with PJ right behind her—intent on finding Grant to make sure Venalda had made it to safety. But as soon as he walked outside, he spotted Carl and his goon squad, who'd joined up with the other oafs in town. The group was having a long-winded strategy session about what kind of weapons they should bring against the forest. Based on the loud back-and-forth, it didn't sound like they were close to agreeing with each other.

"What are they—" PJ started to ask Mary, but he realized with a start that she'd disappeared already.

"Psst!"

PJ jumped, searching for the source of the sound. He finally spotted Benny and his two siblings crouching behind a bush next to the town hall.

"What are you doing here?" PJ asked, glancing once more at Carl to make sure he hadn't been seen before approaching the kids.

"My folks are arguing," Benny said, thumbing back toward the town hall. "I'm sure my dad's gonna get it from her."

"Probably," PJ said with a chuckle. "But why are you hiding in the bushes?"

"Mom told me to take the siblings home," he said, a little uneasy. "I was gonna, but I don't want..." He glanced toward Carl and the rest. "I don't want them to see us."

"They're not going to hurt you," PJ said.

"They might not, but..." His worried gaze went to the sky. "What if those butterflies come back?"

PJ gripped his shoulder. "They're gone. For the moment. And we're going to figure out why they keep coming to town. Promise. You're safe to go home."

He didn't move, biting his lip nervously.

"Why don't I walk you?" PJ said.

Benny brightened and soon enough, the quartet were on their way. PJ would've much rather gone to look for Grant, but the kids looked petrified, and he couldn't blame them. The attack had been so strange, so random, and so intense that it almost seemed a new assailant had come onto the scene.

The closer the group got to the Werst property, the easier Benny seemed to breathe, to the point where he stopped glancing at the sky and joined his brother in throwing rocks at the dirt. Little Margo, who refused to be picked up, was right behind them, laughing riotously as she threw pebbles after her brothers.

"Do you boys ever go to the Pearlwind property?" PJ asked, recalling what Venalda had told him about the children coming close to her wards.

"We play in the woods near there, but we've never gone onto her property, I don't think," Benny said, his brows knitting together. "Dad told us where the line is and said never to cross it."

"Not that we can. Too many vines," Pascal added.

"Have you gone recently?" PJ asked. "Since the attacks started?"

Benny thought for a moment. "The last time I went was with my dad to gather wood for Ms. Wendy's chairs and tables."

PJ slowed, his gaze moving to Mr. Gibbons's yard and the flowers just visible over the fence. "Do you know where Mr. Gibbons got those flowers?"

"No, I think I saw them growing near where we got our wood."

PJ turned, recalling what Quentin had said about fixing his fence the morning of the attack. And Orville, who'd said that Byron had been the one to make the planks for him PJ had used to fix his stand the first time. What if Quentin falling into his stand *wasn't* accidental either?

"Is it the wood?" PJ stammered, turning back to look toward Gilramore.

"What?" Benny asked.

"Can you three run home from here?" PJ asked, putting his hands on their shoulders. "I need to get back to town."

"Okay!" Benny turned to his siblings. "Last one back is a rotten dragon's egg!"

PJ winced at the insinuation, but the threat seemed to put wings on all three kids. Within a minute, they were back on their porch, huffing and puffing. Benny opened the front door and waved before herding the other kids inside.

PJ spun on his heel and ran back toward Gilramore.

"I sure hope Grant's doing what he's supposed to."

PJ sprinted the whole way back to town, which was longer than he'd thought, and by the time he burst into the Gilramore Inn, he had a stitch in his side. Wendy had started sweeping up the remnants of her broken furniture and stared at the teenager as he caught his breath.

"Don't tell me there's another attack," she said with a look.

"Your furniture," PJ said, once he could talk again. "Where'd you get the wood for it?"

"Erm. Byron got it for me."

"Where did *he* get it?" PJ asked.

"You'll have to ask him," Wendy said. "What's going on? What does furniture have to do with anything—"

PJ didn't give her a chance to finish, but ran back out the door and into the square. Carl and his band of goons had finally migrated away from the square, but he spotted two of them in front of the blacksmith shop, so they hadn't yet left to attack the forest. Surely, by now, Grant had gotten through to Venalda and should've been back to the square—but a twinge of unease knotted in PJ's chest when he didn't see his friend anywhere in the square.

"I'll worry about that in a minute," PJ muttered, spotting Orville and Ygritte at the remains of their farm stands.

"What's up? Did you find something?" Ygritte asked as PJ jogged over.

"Orville, those slats we used to make your farm

stand," PJ said, out of breath from all the running, "where did Byron get them? Do you know?"

"The forest, probably," he said with a shrug. "Why? You want to help him get more?"

"No, I—" Abigail was leaving the town hall, her fists balled up and her face tight with anger, so PJ flashed a quick, tense smile to the farmers. "Be right back."

He dashed across the square, earning a scornful look from the former head registrar. "I'd think you'd be smart enough to leave me alone right now. I'm *furious* with my husband—"

"Where'd he go?" PJ asked, looking around.

"I honestly don't know, and I don't care." She shook her head angrily. "I wonder what else he's lied about lately."

"Don't…" PJ eyed her. "Don't be too hard on him. He's a good man. A good father. And I can't say I blame him for wanting to spend time with his son." He gestured. "The whole falling in the creek part wasn't his fault, either."

"I suppose that's how you two got to *talking*, hm?" Abigail said with a glare. "You saved Benny from the river, so he offered you a meal and a bed?"

PJ nodded.

"Well, I'm…" She seemed to realize something and softened, just a hair. "Thank you for saving him."

"Of course," PJ said a little impatiently. "Mr. Gibbons, your neighbor. Where did he get the flowers he was planting?"

"I'm sorry?" Abigail laughed. "What does that..." Her face grew slack. "You don't think it's... We've been gathering things in that forest for years. Byron's always gone there to harvest wood. We've never had a problem."

"So Mr. Gibbons got his flowers from the forest, too?" PJ asked.

"I don't know for sure, but I think so... He did mention he'd been in the forest earlier that day," Abigail said, as if the conversation were ridiculous. "I know you're trying to help, but there's no way—"

"Peej!" Grant called, running toward the group. "You gotta come help. I'm not sure she's heard me. I hollered and yelled and tried to get through the vines, and they kicked me out." He swallowed hard, looking very much like he regretted his failure. "I'm so sorry. I tried as hard as I could. But I didn't know where Carl—"

"They haven't left yet," PJ said. "Thankfully."

"Get through to whom?" Abigail asked as Ygritte and Orville walked over to join the conversation.

PJ ignored Abigail's question. "Ygritte, is there another way to get to the Pearlwind property? One that doesn't go along the main road?"

"I know of a way, but it might be overgrown," Ygritte said. "Why?"

"We need to warn Venalda," PJ said.

"She's back?" Abigail gasped. "What do you mean *warn* her? She's the one attacking the town, isn't she?"

"No," PJ said. "Someone else is—I think someone who's mad about you, I don't know, taking wood and plants out of the forest."

"Sounds like something Venalda would be mad about," Ygritte said.

"We were with her when this last attack started," Grant said plainly. "But she's closed off her property now. She isn't listening to me."

"That's good, then," Ygritte said. "Maybe that's enough to keep Carl from getting through."

As if summoned, Carl walked out of the blacksmith shop, followed by three other farmers and five soldiers—all clad in iron armor, carrying axes and swords. The extra weight seemed quite difficult to bear, as they moved slowly, rocking from side to side with a meandering sort of gait.

"Let's…go…!" Carl huffed and puffed, clearly out of practice fighting against magical foes.

"How did the queen win again?" PJ muttered.

"Maybe the magical people were very, very slow," Grant replied.

"I can show you the way to the Pearlwind

property," Abigail said, her face unreadable. "There's a path right by my house. But there's a clear delineation. You won't be able to get onto the property."

"Peej has his ways," Grant said.

"I'm coming, too," Ygritte announced. "Orville, you too. Maybe seeing a pair of friendly faces will help her lower her defenses."

"Either way," Grant said, nodding toward the slow-moving armada plodding across the town square. "we *probably* should get moving."

~

It seemed Benny wasn't the only Werst used to traipsing through the wooded property. Abigail moved swiftly, knowing exactly which way to turn and which rocks marked the correct direction. PJ still wasn't sure what she was thinking; was she angry about the witches being there or was there something else behind her gaze? She wasn't being very chatty, so PJ didn't ask.

"Well?" Abigail said as they came upon what appeared to be a tall hedge maze that ran parallel to where they stood as far as the eye could see. "Here it is."

"Let me try," Ygritte said, as PJ took a step forward. She cleared her throat. "Venalda? Honey? It's Ygritte. From town. Are you…" Her voice grew thick. "Are you really alive in there? Are you safe?" A tear fell down her cheek. "After all this time?"

The vines twisted and moved, earning a gasp of surprise from Abigail.

PJ steadied her with a hand on her shoulder and a nod. "I think it's—"

The vines snapped loudly together, tightening their hold.

"She must've strengthened her wards," PJ said, with a sigh. "I don't think it's wise for us to break them—not with Sir Ironhead and his merry men on their way."

"So what do we do?" Grant said. "I already tried yelling at her. All the vines did was grow thicker and swat at me."

"Do you think she heard you, or…?"

Grant shook his head. "Maybe we can break the wards and—"

"You'd better not break *anything* with those idiots coming this way." Mary appeared from behind nearby bushes, looking wild and irate.

"M-Mary?" Abigail sputtered. "What are you—"

"You knew she was here, didn't you?" PJ glared at her. "This whole time."

"Of course I knew," Mary said. "And I was doing everything I could to keep you two idiots from spilling the beans to the rest of town to avoid exactly this scenario—Carl and a mob with iron weapons marching this way to set fire to the forest and smoke out an innocent woman."

PJ opened and closed his mouth, warmth coming to his cheeks. "Oh."

"Mary, you can't... You've been harboring a magical fugitive?" Abigail said, looking at her sister-in-law as if she'd never seen her before. "Byron doesn't..."

"Of course he knows," Mary said gently. "He's the one who helped me save her."

Abigail's mouth fell open.

"Where is he?" Ygritte asked.

"He's inside, helping her test her wards," Mary said. "Which is what I was doing when I heard you about to blow another hole in her vines. Do you know how hard it was for her to fix them? Not just the vines, of course, but the magic? She's still trying to get the threads back together."

"Mary, how could you?" Abigail was crying. "How could you two lie to me all these years? We worked for the queen, we—" She shook her head. "My children live here."

"Venalda wouldn't hurt your children, Abby," Mary said gently. "In fact, she's—"

"You went to her about the butterflies, didn't you?" PJ finished for her. "She's the one you spoke with."

"Whatever's sending these things into town is doing so outside the bounds of her magic," Mary replied. "And she will be *happy* to continue looking into it, once strange young men stop coming into town and mucking things up."

"She should've just been honest with us," Grant said. "We told her we came in peace."

"I'm *very* confused," Orville said, rubbing the back of his neck. "Mary, you were the mayor. The queen appointed you. You're the ones who *brought* the registrar's office here. Why would—"

"It's precisely because of those soldiers that it was so safe, paradoxically," Mary said "Byron and I told them the witches had been cleared out. Byron led the arrests, in fact. Because... well..." She chuckled. "He was able to get them to safety."

"But why? The queen outlawed magic because it's dangerous," Abigail said.

"The Pearlwinds aren't dangerous."

Byron's voice echoed from somewhere unseen, and to their left, the vines and tangles pulled away, revealing the tall man and Venalda next to him. Ygritte let out a cry of happiness and ran toward the witch, almost tackling her.

"You're alive!" she sobbed, perhaps much louder than she should have, holding the witch's face. "Oh, goodness gracious, you're alive!"

"Byron, what is..." Abigail said, ignoring the reunion. "I don't understand."

"I grew up with Venalda," he said, gesturing to

her. "And her siblings. They were my friends. They weren't dangerous, or evil, or whatever else the queen might've thought. I could give some leeway for wizards and the powerful ones, but the witches who lived here?" He shook his head. "I knew if I got them to safety, they'd never hurt another person. And they haven't." He nodded to Venalda, who was still holding Ygritte as she sobbed. "Remember when Pascal had that nasty sickness last year?"

"Yes, and you went to…" Abigail shook her head. "You got magic?"

"Venalda made him a tincture," Byron said. "She's been watching over the boys when they come into the forest. She loves them as much as… Well, as much as we do." He took his wife's hands. "I'm sorry I never told you. I should've told you the moment the queen's regime fell, but—"

"Carl," Mary said with a sneer. "That ogre."

"If word got out that there was a magical person living here, he'd stop at nothing… Well, you already see what he's doing," Byron said.

"Because there've been attacks on our town," Abigail said, though there wasn't as much fire behind it. "You were attacked, Byron."

"I swear, that wasn't me," Venalda said, holding up her hands. "I don't know who it is."

"Who lives in the forest near your house?" PJ asked. "Because that's who's been attacking the town. It all makes sense." He pointed to Byron. "You've been getting your wood from this part of the forest, haven't you? For the furniture? Your fence? All of it?"

"Well, erm… Yeah." Byron looked around. "But I've always gotten the wood from here."

"Burt Gibbons got flowers, Quentin got wood for a fence, Orville got planks, Wendy got wood from Byron," PJ ticked off his fingers. "Someone's mad that you're getting stuff from the forest."

"Who would be mad about that?" Venalda asked. "There's no one—"

"*I am!*"

Everyone looked around, unsure where the voice was coming from until they spotted a gold-winged creature fluttering in from above. But it wasn't a butterfly; it was a human with wings.

"A fairy?" PJ blurted. "What—"

The fairy landed on the branches of a nearby tree, marching out and pointing at each of those gathered, his voice so high-pitched it almost hurt PJ's ears.

"You nasty little humans have been *poaching* wood from *my* forest! First, that monster took my flowers. *My flowers!* The ones *I planted!* Do you know that fairies eat the nectar from flowers, too?

I'd planted them from seed, then that ogre comes traipsing in here and ripping them out to plant on *his* property? I think *not!*"

Grant let out a bark of disbelief.

"Then I see, I see *my wood* being used for *a fence*. My wood! The wood *I've* been growing all this time to make my home in. Do you know how long it takes to grow a tree big enough to live in? Hm? Do you?"

The fairy had lifted off the tree branch and started haranguing Byron directly now.

"And you just walk in and *cut down my tree!* I couldn't believe it. So you cut down my tree, I mess up your face." He bristled, a bit of fairy dust falling to the ground. "But…well, I didn't mean for your boy to fall in the river. I'm quite sorry for that and grateful he's safe."

"T-thank you?" Byron said, unable to tear his gaze from the tiny creature. "H-how long…?"

"How long have you lived in this forest?" Venalda asked.

"My whole life!" he bellowed. "Well, I did have to spend a few years in hiding when that nasty queen was in charge, but now I'm back, and I'm *disgusted* at the damage to my property."

Byron, Mary, and Venalda shared a curious look. "We've lived here our entire lives and never seen you," Mary said.

"Well, I do keep to myself. I did even in the before times," he said with an indignant sniff. "But you monsters never got too far into my territory either."

"I…" Byron cleared his throat, redness coming to his cheeks. "A week ago, Mr. Gibbons told me about a thick copse of oak trees that would be useful for rebuilding Wendy's tables. Said it was in a clearing, and he wasn't quite sure how such mature trees…" He let out a breath and looked at the sky. "Oh, my goodness."

"My goodness is right!" the fairy squeaked.

"So you've been mad that people cut down your oak trees," PJ said with a little laugh. "And pulled up your flowers. And that's why you've gotten the butterflies all riled up to attack people?"

"Yes. You've got to fight fire with fire. I hoped you would get the message, but then *this one* traipsing around my clearing again." He pointed to PJ. "Nasty dragon you are."

PJ's brows rose as the group stared at him. "You know what I am?"

"I saw you burn a hole in this witch's hedges," he said with a glare. "Saw the amulet. I've crossed paths with a few of you before."

PJ's heart soared. "You have? Where? Where can I find them?"

"This was ages ago. In the before times. I'm sure

they were..." The fairy turned his whole body toward Abigail. "Taken."

The hope deflated as quickly as it had appeared, and Grant squeezed PJ's shoulder comfortingly.

"So, if we stop poaching your wood, you'll stop attacking the town?" Mary asked.

"Obviously."

Let him attack again. Carl.

"Wait, no. We need you to attack one more time," PJ said, an idea coming to him in a flash.

"What?" The Gilramore group turned to PJ in a single movement.

"What in the world?" Ygritte said.

"We've already got to rebuild again," Orville said. "What are you—"

"Not attack the town, but..." PJ smiled slyly. "There's a group of slow-moving soldiers who need some encouragement to leave Gilramore."

"A flock of butterflies isn't going to do much," Byron said. "I mean, it hasn't scared him yet."

"That's because it hasn't attacked him yet," PJ pointed out. "Men like that are always overcompensating for their cowardice." He met Grant's gaze with a smirk. "I have an idea. But it's going to take all of us—Venalda, me, erm... What's your name?"

"Ichibald," the fairy replied. "I don't see why I should help. You lot have done nothing but ruin my forest."

"I'll get the flowers back to you," Byron said. "And I can't rebuild the trees, but if you needed a temporary house built, I'd be happy to do that, too."

"And you can have access to my fruits and vegetables," Venalda said. "They're in season all year long, too."

Ichibald seemed to consider this deal. "Who, exactly, are we trying to scare?"

"He's a menace to the town," Mary said. "Anti-magic. It's in your best interest for him to leave, as well. He's..." She looked at Byron. "He's actually the one who told Burt where to find the flowers."

"Y-yeah," Byron said with a nod. "Yeah, Carl found them first. And I don't know if he'd listen if we told him to avoid the clearing, now that he knows—"

"Fine, fine, fine," Ichibald said with a harrumph. "I'll help. You want butterflies or something else?"

"I have something in mind," PJ said, meeting Grant's gaze with a smirk. "But you guys are gonna have to play along. If you're up for it." He looked at Abigail, who'd been quiet since the fairy made his appearance. "I need your help, too, Abigail."

"Me?" She blanched. "What do you need me for?"

"You were his boss," PJ said. "So you'd know

which of his kingside soldiers would scare him the most."

She opened her mouth in surprise. "I think I know of one that could work, yes." She looked around. "But we're really going to use magic to…" She licked her lips, having a quick think to herself. "You know what? Fine. He's a bully anyway. And I won't worry about the boys walking home from school by themselves after he's gone." She looked at PJ. "Are you sure you know what you're doing?"

"Not at all," PJ said with a laugh as he met Grant's approving smirk. "But Grant does have *some* experience with causing diversions. So I'm sure we can come up with something good."

~

By the time the trap was set, the slow-moving parade of iron-clad soldiers had made it to the perimeter of the Pearlwind property. Of course, no one wanted to be the first to approach the thick tangle of vines and branches, which gave PJ and the others time to put the finishing touches on their plan.

"Are you sure about this?" Venalda asked, holding up her hands.

"Yeah," PJ said, with a nod to Grant. "Do it."

Venalda covered them in her glamour, the magic sticking to PJ's skin with a slimy sort of feeling. Grant, too, made a face as it covered his body, but let out a gasp when he noticed his arm, which now bore a gaping, bleeding wound.

"Goodness," he said, flapping it around. "That looks awful."

"You should see your face," Byron said with a frown. "You look like you've seen the wrong end of a sucker punch."

"We have to make it look like we're losing," PJ said, glancing down at his own body. His clothes were burned, and his shoe had fallen off. "Okay, is everyone ready?"

"I'm still not sure this is going to work," Mary said with a scowl. "But yes, we're ready."

PJ nodded to Grant, and the two burst from the forest, limping and howling. "G-get out of h-here!" PJ bellowed, clutching his leg, which looked like it had seen the bad end of a fireball.

"What's going on?" Carl said, his armor *clink-clink-clinking* as he meandered over. "What happened to you?"

"W-we found the culprit," Grant said, gasping for breath with fear etched on his face. "The one who's been attacking the town."

"Why are you burned?" one of the farmers asked.

"It was a t-trap," PJ said. "They brought…they brought a dragon shifter with them."

"They? Who's *they*?" Carl demanded.

"Look out!" PJ cried.

Venalda's vines had broken free of the bounds of the property and were creeping toward the crowd of iron-clad soldiers. One of Carl's goons hoisted his ax down on it, cutting it in half. But before he even lifted the blade again, another took its place. Creeping, crawling, twisting toward the soldiers.

"What's happening?" another farmer asked, inching backward.

"Who's *they*?" Carl growled, baring his teeth at PJ and Grant.

"He called himself E-Edgar," PJ said with a breathy sigh. "He said… He said he sent the butterflies to draw you out, Carl."

Carl's eyes widened. "Edgar?"

"He said…" Grant continued, clutching his arm and wincing. "He said now that the queen was gone… He said you were to pay for your crimes."

Carl swallowed, the blood draining from his face. He backed up a step, right into one of the farmers, who pushed back.

"What are you so scared of?" the farmer bellowed. "You said we'd be safe wearing this iron armor!"

"Y-yeah, of course," Carl said, though he hadn't shaken off the fear in his eyes. "Yeah. We're going in! You two boys stay out of the way. Obviously didn't learn anything from Dag Flanigan. Made a mess of things. I'm not afraid of any ol' soldier or anything with—"

PJ spotted Ygritte in the brush and gave her a brief nod. She opened a clay vase magicked to capture PJ's dragon roar, which echoed into the clearing. Even PJ got chills.

"W-what is that...?" another farmer said, dropping his sword.

"Pick up your weapon," Carl snarled. "There's nothing—there aren't any more dragon shifters—"

Ichibald released a flurry of butterflies, which zoomed directly toward the soldiers. They yelped in fear and dropped the rest of their weapons, running back to town as fast as their feet would carry them.

"Carl, you have to run!" PJ cried, sounding as if the world were ending. "They said they won't rest until *all* the queen's soldiers account for their crimes."

"Let me go!" Byron cried from the woods. "I've done nothing wrong!"

"You awful creature," Abigail's voice rang out, sounding like she was being manhandled. "You have *no* idea who I am! I'm the head registrar of Gilramore. And you will unhand me!"

"Please!" It was Mary's turn to chime in. "Please, they have children. Please let them go!"

"You're all under arrest for crimes against the king," Venalda, who'd magicked her voice to sound different, said. "Come quietly, and we won't have to hurt you."

Orville opened another clay vase, and PJ's roar echoed out through the clearing again. Venalda sent more vines slithering toward Carl, growing thorns as they reached for him.

"Come on, you stupid oafs," Grant muttered under his breath. "Take the bait."

PJ pushed himself to stand, taking a deep breath. "I'm going back in. Come with me if you dare. But I'm *not* letting those awful kingside monsters take those kids' parents from them."

He squared his shoulders and ran back into the forest until he was sure he was fully hidden. Grant moaned, crying about how sad he was that his best friend was going to die, begging the woods to release PJ, but Carl seemed frozen in place, his hands twisting around his weapons. The other two were similarly stuck, though the farmers had dropped all their iron armor on the road as they'd retreated.

"Okay, time for Plan B," PJ said, pulling his amulet from his shirt. "Everyone stand back."

Tim roared to life in his mind, and when he opened his mouth, the sound that came out was even louder than what Venalda had captured in the vases. Smoke pooled from his mouth as he inhaled and exhaled deeply, and pinpricks itched his back, as if his wings were waiting to emerge.

I could do it, he thought. *I could go full dragon. That would scare them off.*

He opened his mouth, and a tunnel of fire billowed out, aimed directly at Carl and his goons. Despite the heavy iron, they dropped to the ground before the fire hit them, though PJ was pretty sure they'd lost some of their hair. When he closed his mouth, there was another black tunnel of burned plants. Venalda's magic descended on him again, making him appear six inches taller, with blond hair and a chiseled chin. The red eyes remained visible, however, as PJ's gaze locked on Carl's.

"L-Let's get out of here!"

The first of the three ripped off his armor and hightailed it away from Gilramore, with the second not too far behind him. But Carl—stupid, stubborn oaf that he was—was frozen to the spot.

"You know," PJ said, his voice mixing with Tim's, "they told me to bring you back. But wouldn't it be a shame if I told them how you'd resisted arrest?" He chuckled menacingly. "Isn't that what you used to tell your soldiers? No one would care if they complained?"

The insinuation was quite clear, and finally, *finally,* Carl let out a scream of fear, ripped off all his armor, and ran off toward the south.

No one breathed for a good five minutes, then Grant pushed himself upright and said, "Well, I do believe I deserve an award for my dramatic portrayal of 'guy about to die by dragon shifter.'"

PJ let out a laugh, which came with a plume of smoke. But Tim willingly returned to his slumber deep in PJ's mind, and PJ felt like himself. He turned to the rest of the group and winced.

"I'm sorry about your plants, Venalda." He cleared his throat. "Again."

"They'll regrow," she said, keeping her distance. Abigail, Byron, and Mary, too, looked at PJ as if he were dangerous.

Which he supposed he probably was, after that display.

"I'm still me," he said, blinking away the burning in his eyes. "I hope I didn't scare you too much, but I was trying to get a point across."

"I'll say you did that," Mary said. "Stroke of genius to use his own words against him. At least he knows what it feels like to be afraid."

"I can't believe I let you eat at my dinner table," Abigail said, her voice breathy and terrified. "And speak to my boys, and—"

PJ frowned, but Grant stepped up and patted him on the shoulder. "Just like Venalda here, PJ only uses his powers for good. Not everyone with magic is out to hurt people. In fact, Peej is probably the *best* person to be a dragon shifter. If I had it," he made a noise, winking at PJ, "they'd probably never get me outta the gold hoard."

"You didn't really work for Dag Flanigan, did you?" Mary said with a look.

"No, he was in Pigsend to find me, actually," PJ said with a chuckle. "Glad he didn't."

"Me, too," Byron replied. "Otherwise, we'd have been stuck with Carl forever."

"Why did you come to town?" Abigail said.

"I'm looking for more of my kind," PJ said. "My dragon, erm… Well, he's the one who sensed Benny was in trouble. I'm not sure if staying was the right thing to do for the task I've been given but…"

"We're grateful," Venalda said with a smile as she locked arms with Ygritte. "Now, I don't know about you, but I'm *very* interested to see what this innkeeper has for dinner. Anyone else famished?"

Chapter Twenty Two

Dinner was a raucous affair, with the farmers who *hadn't* gone to attack Venalda coming to the inn. Wendy was happy to meet the witch, and even happier to find out she wasn't the one sending butterflies to attack the town.

"A fairy?" She blinked. "In our forest?"

"As strange as it sounds," Abigail said with a laugh. She'd gone home to retrieve the children and brought them to the inn, and they were happily dunking pieces of thick bread their father had baked into the venison stew Wendy had made. Of course, there was nowhere to sit, as the butterflies had destroyed all the furniture, so everyone was cross-legged on the floor.

"So we're okay with magic?" Wendy asked her and Mary.

"The king's on the throne," Mary said. "It's legal."

"What about Carl?"

"I don't think he's going to be a problem," Mary replied with a look at PJ. "And if he is, we'll be sure to tell him he's no longer welcome. I'm tired of living in fear of him."

"Hear, hear," Orville said, his husband sitting beside him. "But there is all the damage to fix." He glanced at PJ. "Are you two leaving, or are you going to stick around and help us rebuild?"

"I think we can stay another day or two," Grant said before PJ could speak. "I bet I could even swing a hammer."

"Can you now?" PJ asked. "That's new."

"I'm a new man, Peej," he said, puffing out his chest. "You know, there is something to this saving-the-town stuff. Makes a person feel good about themselves."

"Yeah, I agree," PJ said, looking around.

Abigail sat with her children and Byron, who was deep in conversation with his sister and Venalda. The former head registrar still looked uncomfortable with magic so close, but that she was sitting with her (and even letting her children be in the same room as PJ) was a good sign. She met PJ's gaze and gave him a little wave.

"I think we've left this town in better shape than we found it, for sure."

"Minus all the destruction," Grant said with a snort. "You know, you really can be terrifying when you want to be."

"I don't try to be," PJ said, a blush coming to his cheek. "But I do feel like Tim and I have come to an understanding." He lowered his voice. "You know, back in the forest, I felt like I was about to shift. But I was able to stop it. Maybe…Maybe I could do it one day. And get back to myself."

"Best not to test that theory until we hear back from the grannies," he said, giving PJ a look. "You *did* write to them, didn't you?"

He nodded. "But who knows when they'll get it —or get back to me." He took another bite of his stew. "But I don't feel like I don't know what I'm doing anymore. And we'll get back on the road soon enough."

~

Gilramore was filled with a renewed sense of purpose. The next morning, PJ was awoken by the sounds of hammering. He peered out the window to find Orville, Toby, and a few others already starting on the farm stands.

"Well, shall we get to it?" PJ asked, turning to

Grant, who was just waking up.

"Why is your amulet glowing?" Grant asked.

"What?" PJ looked down, his heart pounding as he realized his amulet was glowing bright white—like it was about to catch fire.

Without thinking, he yanked it from around his neck and threw it on the floor. The light turned from white to pulsing red, and PJ winced as he scrambled backward, unsure what was going to happen next.

A ghost-like, translucent hand jutted out from the amulet, followed by an arm then a bunch of bluish-gray hair. "Budge up, Janet, I can't get through."

Another hand appeared, shoving the head that was coming out to the side. "Let me get through, Rita. I need to get my bearings."

"Wait for me!" This time, a foot came first, landing on the hardwood floor of the inn, followed by a leg. "Wait, I'm facing the wrong way. Janet, help me out."

"Sure thing, Gladys." The foot disappeared, and a head with silver hair appeared. "There you go, love."

"Thanks, Janet."

PJ gaped at the sight of the three grannies, who were still half inside the amulet, but were peering up at him like a trio of ghosts. They adjusted their hair then each other's clothing then finally seemed to realize PJ and Grant were gaping at them.

"Hello, dears!" Janet, with the almost-blue hair, waved at PJ. "You're looking quite well. And you've grown so much since we last saw you!"

"So sorry to hear about university," Rita tutted, adjusting a lock of her red hair. "But I always say, these things happen for a reason. It was just good timing, you know."

"Where are we, anyway?" Gladys asked, looking around the inn.

PJ finally remembered his manners. "H-hi, Grannies. You're… What is this?"

"Oh, didn't we tell you?" Janet said. "The amulet provides a quick way to chat with us, if ever you're in need."

"Never needed to use it myself," Rita said with a chuckle. "As everyone I ever needed to talk to was within arm's reach."

"Could've used it a few times," Gladys said with a look. "But we're happy you have it. Sorry we didn't mention it sooner."

"Y-yeah, there's a lot you didn't mention," PJ said. "Like how I can talk to my dragon now?"

"Oh, yes!" Janet clapped. "We were hoping you wanted to talk about that. Your letter was so vague."

"Probably for the best," Gladys said. "The world's not quite as safe as it ought to be, even with the king back in power."

"Did you know he was living in Pigsend?" Rita said. "Absolutely blew our minds. Wonder what other secrets your quaint little town was hiding."

"But you had a question for us, dear?" Janet said.

The three grannies smiled expectantly at PJ.

"Well, Peej?" Grant said, gesturing to him. "Go on."

So PJ told them what had happened in Gilramore, and it was actually lovely to be able to talk freely and share every detail without worrying he was inadvertently spilling a secret. The grannies listened intently, smiling as if he were telling them about a nice round of cards he'd won, until he got to the part about his dragon nearly coming out.

"Oh, PJ, you absolutely cannot shift," Janet said, her voice taking on an uncommon note of worry. "You're far too young. Too inexperienced."

Gladys nodded. "It would be bad for everyone involved."

"But Tim, erm, my dragon, he seems so…" PJ didn't know how to phrase it. "I don't think he'd let me do anything awful, would he?"

"Darling, your dragon benefits from your human mind the same way you benefit from his dragon magic," Rita said patiently. "Once the human mind is gone, the dragon will be free to do whatever he wants. It's not a good thing."

"Dragon shifters are supposed to move in packs precisely because we need each other to keep a handle on the magic, should we transform," Janet said. "And while we are so happy you've got a good friend in Grant, he's nowhere near equipped to handle you if you lose control."

"The amulet will help," Rita said. "But it won't stop a shift completely, if you let it get too far."

PJ shivered, nodding. "I won't do it again. I'm sorry."

"Nothing to be sorry about, darling!" Janet laughed. "You're learning. It appears we forgot to put *that* in the letter."

"In our defense, it's the first time we've ever had to write such a letter," Gladys said.

"I wonder what else we forgot?" Rita said, tapping her finger to her chin. "Oh, I'm sure it'll come out eventually."

PJ shared a look with Grant, who cleared his throat and knelt beside his friend. "Erm, I guess the *real* question we had for you three is…well, should we have stayed and figured out what was going on? Should we have gotten involved with Carl and the rest? Or should we have just moved on when we realized there wasn't a shifter here in town?"

"Oh, dear sweethearts, you absolutely did the right thing by staying," Rita said with a nod.

"If a town needs your help, dragon shifter or not, you should help," Gladys said.

"You've been given such a wonderful gift, PJ," Janet said. "And this world has so many problems that could use someone with your abilities. To not use them to help, well, that's more of a crime than anything else."

The tension PJ had held in his chest for days finally loosened, and he smiled in relief.

"You see, Peej? I told you we were right to stick around," Grant said, puffing out his chest. "We gotta help people when they need help."

"Oh, you said that, did you?" PJ said, rolling his eyes before turning to the grannies. "One more question: What's the deal with the amulet giving us gold when we do good?"

"When you do…?" Janet frowned. "It should just give you what you need."

"Darn thing is busted." Rita reached down and knocked the amulet a few times. In response, it spat out five gold coins and a large ruby. "There. Must've just been clogged."

Grant whimpered, and PJ was sure he was about to swoon.

"It should give you what you need to be able to travel the country," Janet said. "Though, we often found we needed less gold than we thought, especially as we do good things wherever we go. I'm sure you've found the same."

PJ nodded. Wendy had told them they could stay as long as they wanted at the inn. "Thank you," he said. "And thank you for…well, for responding. I wasn't sure if I was bothering you—"

"Not at *all*, love," Rita said with a cheery wave.

"We're spending time in the hot springs near the dragon cave," Gladys said. "It's wonderful on the bones."

Rita beamed. "You boys should spend some time there if you come to visit."

"We hope you'll come to visit soon," Janet finished. "But don't worry if you get sidetracked. As we said in our letter, we searched the country for seven years looking for our kind, and you were the only one we found. That's a lot of houses to fix and towns to put right. And we ended up finding you at just the right time, too!"

PJ couldn't argue with that. "Any idea where I should go next?"

"Just keep following the road, dear," Janet said. "Something's bound to pop up."

"It always does," Gladys said with a cheery smile.

Knowing he had the blessing and support of the grannies for whatever he did, PJ spent the next two days helping the folks of Gilramore get back to normal. But on the third day, when everything was back to normal, he rose feeling rather melancholy to leave Gilramore behind. But, as he peered out into the rebuilt farmer's market, he knew his work here was finished. There was, as Grant kept saying, another town down the road who might have a spate of frogs, or an infestation of lizards, or maybe, if he was lucky, a dragon shifter.

But if not, he would keep doing what he thought was right. And that was the most freeing feeling of all.

Word spread quickly that the boys were leaving, and almost half the town crowded into the Gilramore Inn to say goodbye. Benny had tears in his eyes as he hugged PJ's legs tightly, and even Margo waved goodbye to him from the safety of her father's arms.

"You take care of your siblings, all right?" PJ said to the little boy. "Listen to your father. And please avoid the creek when the water's high."

He nodded and squeezed again before his father took his place, pulling PJ *and* Grant in for bear hugs. When he was done, Abigail kissed both their cheeks.

"So you're okay with having a witch living next door?" PJ asked.

"I'm not happy that Byron lied to me all this time," she said. "But...well, the world's changed.

Suppose I'd better get used to it."

"That seems…" Grant eyed her. "Like a big change of heart."

She huffed. "Well, I'm not completely fine with it. But I know what's in my husband's heart. If he thinks she can be trusted, then I can…learn to trust her, too." The way she glanced back at the witch told PJ that was going to take a *long* time, but at least she was willing.

"What are you going to do now that the queen's gone?" PJ asked.

"Byron and I were talking," Abigail said, sharing a look of amusement with her husband. "He's gotten *so* good at making bread lately, and since it's been made quite clear that there's no bakery in town to provide sweets to my *poor* deprived children…"

"You're going to open one?" PJ said with a grin.

"We're going to explore the possibility," Abigail said. "The registrar's office is no longer in use, of course, so we could turn it into something else. I'm going to write to the…*king*…" She said the word as if it pained her. "To send some funds to do it. I hear they're eager to fix what was broken. So maybe they can help revitalize our town."

"Sounds like a great idea," PJ said. "I hope they send what you need."

Mary was up next, hugging them as tightly as her brother. "Thank you for everything. I'm so sorry for all the misdirection and whatnot. But I think you can understand why."

PJ nodded. "Any word from Carl?"

"Toby went down as far as Padstow to look for him." She smirked. "There was talk of a trio of scared-looking queen's soldiers who were asking about passage out of the country."

"Hopefully he won't darken your doors again," PJ said.

Ygritte and Venalda were next, hugging PJ so tightly he couldn't breathe. The witch turned to gesture behind her, where a pair of unfamiliar people stood. "I wanted to introduce my siblings. Inez and my brother Garrett."

PJ's mouth fell open as he shook their hands. "What…where have they been? Not here, right?"

"No." Venalda's eyes grew wet as she stared at them. "They were hiding in an underground haven near Cheshireville. But they're back now, and we're so…" She sighed. "So happy that we can be with our friends and our town once again. We owe you so much, PJ."

"You don't owe me a thing," he said. "I'm just here to help."

Venalda took PJ's hand and squeezed it, pulling him close and nodding toward the amulet on his chest.

"You've got some power in there. You know

that, right?" She pulled him in closer. "Be careful with it."

"I know," he said. "I had a chat with my grandmothers."

"Good."

The last to say goodbye were Orville and Toby, who provided no fewer than five pounds of apples each for the boys to take with them. PJ thanked them for their generosity, while Grant seemed to already dread the idea of hauling them around until they reached the next town.

"Where to next?" Abigail asked.

"Wherever the road takes us, I suppose," PJ said. "Maybe we'll head down to Padstow. Anything interesting about that place?"

"Lots of gnomes," Mary said. "Erm, they were okay by the queen because they harvested magic."

"I'm positive we won't find a single magical problem there, then," Grant said, hoisting his apple-laden bag. "But we really should get a move on if we want to get there before dark."

"Right." PJ turned to the crowd, scanning their faces one more time. And then, with a final wave, he walked out the door and hit the road with Grant, wondering what adventures waited for them next.

PJ continues his adventures in

${A}$CKNOWLEGMENTS

As always, first thanks goes to my husband, for supporting me, believing in me, and being my rock during the difficult season of two very small children and me trying to take on the world. Thanks must also go to my parents, my in-laws, and my aunt for being the world's best village and allowing me to keep writing with said very small children.

Thanks to Chelsea, Danielle, Lisa, and Lacey for being the all-star team who helps bring these beautiful books to life.

Thanks go to the Sush Street Team for being the cheerleaders who love these books and continue to read everything I put out.

And finally, and most ardently, thanks to you, the reader, for buying, loving, and sharing my cozy little stories about Bev, Lillie, and now PJ. I'm so grateful I stumbled into this wonderful niche, and that it's brought you as much joy as it's brought me.

Kickstarter Thank You

A special thank you to the backers who supported the Firewing Investigations Kickstarter:

Dominic Chiavassa, RL Sarty, Becca Reppert, Kate Ehrenholm, Rik Geuze, Megan Walton, Ceillie Simkiss, Megan Luchs, Liz Delton, Tiffanie Drayton, Liz Semkiu, Eriko, Becky flores, Maddie Clements, Christina Simmers, John Idlor, Wineke Sloos, Annarose Willhite, Renee Meeks, Bethany Darity, Brock M, Antoinetta Aquila, Sarah B., Yngve J. K. Hestem, Paul J Lawrence, n/a, Timm, Megan Sanborn, Caledonia, Wren Jones, Bryan Fulton, Terry Steinke, Catherine Holmes, Astridd, April Vaughn, Stephanie Cranford, Cortney Babcock, Rowan Stone, Rebecca Buchanan, leave it blank!, Silver, Rae McFarron, CJ Evans, Chase McGlinchey, Susan Henry, Corrie Pelc, Paul Cleaveland, Jim Landis, The Booches, E. R. Paskey, Jessica Hoyal, Shawn Adair, pjk, Michael J. Anderson, Christy S, Laura M, Mellissa Boslow, Franchesca Caram, Jaci, Riley Quinn, Natalie Munford, Lynn, Stephanie Horn, Sarah Kolar, Inessa Sage, Sheila G., Chris McGee, Kira Bolding,

AK Momster, Victoria P, Lee Larsen, Katherine Brown, Sarah Sabin, Dale A Russell, Julie McGhee, Zephyr Mini, Rachel Green, K.Q. Kimler, Allee Snyder, Kat Fey Diehl, Kat Healy, Gina Lucas, Jennifer Brown, Meaghan Ventura, Penny Lane Walker, Undomiel_ddc, Samantha Newberry, Nora Fritsch, David Holzborn, Heather, Jonathon Mast, polinchka, Stacy Carroll, Delphine L., Maggie G., Chelsea, Allen W. Shepherd, Nadine Ward, Alisha, Jess Gisler, J.J. Irwin, Alyssa Benson, Lynne Freeman, Josefine B., Clarissa, Renee P, Amber O'Donnell, Amanda Balter, Sam Potter, Alexander Hale, Luci D, Charlotte U. P., J. Thomas, TJ Stevenson, Rhonda Goodman, Devon Hood, Iina Kilkki, Anthony Atthowe, Rhonda Parrish, Charlotte Tate, Samantha Ghormley, Molly Harbridge, Sara Liming, Erin Layne, Nikkii Thompson, Megan Allen, Rebecca Batterbee, Holly Niemann, Eddie Joo, Kevin Chevez, Nichole Heydenburg, Alexandra Corrsin, Brian Van Vliet, no name, thank you, Terri Connor, curleyboy, Moth Williams, Michelle Glover, Yoliany Baez, Kate T, Kelly Knight, Simon Mark de Wolfe, Erin Michaud, Lara Adrienne Wong, Paige Massingale, Joshua Gerdes, Julia Byers, Herman Steuernagel, Elaine Canyon, Eileen, Lisa Henson, Daniel Falco, Keric, Richard S. Thomas, Emerald Bruce, Becca Stillo, Dave M, Elizabeth Fiedler, Erin M, Jennifer L.

Pierce, Alicia Foley, Andy McAllister, Marine L., Ike Day, Kyo Carter, Claire Smith-Simmons, Rhonda "Wren" Bender, Laura Nelson, Sean Bradley, Christina M Fernandez, Foxxilfox, Madeline A, Kristin Wallin, Jan B, HeckRaiser, J M Feathers, Jessica Armstrong, Eris, Skye Sisk, Aaron Jamieson, Brent Kerr, Inkprint Press

A MER-MURDER AT THE COVE, A PARANORMAL COZY MYSTERY SERIES

Jo Maelstrom's avoidance problems hit an all-time high when, after weeks of dodging her grandmother's calls, she got a text that "Big Jo" had died suddenly. Now back in Eldred's Hollow, a supernatural haven on the Gulf Coast of Alabama, Jo is forced to reckon with her past – and the severe lack of magic that sent her running in the first place. Her grandmother's bar and marina, Witch's Cove, is in some dire financial straits, and there's more than a few people itching to take it off her hands. But when the leader of the local mermaid clan washes up dead on the shore, Jo finds herself embroiled in the question of who and why – and does it have anything to do with her own grandmother's mysterious death?

A Mer-Murder at the Cove is the first book in the Witch's Cove Paranormal Cozy Mystery series. Available in eBook and Paperback

Also By The Author

EMPATH

Lauren Dailey is in break-up hell, but if you ask her she's doing just great. She hears a mysterious voice promising an easy escape from her problems and finds herself in a brand new world where she has the power to feel what others are feeling. Just one problem—there's a dragon in the mountains that happens to eat Empaths. And it might be the source of the mysterious voice tempting her deeper into her own darkness.

Empath is a stand-alone fantasy available now in eBook, Paperback, and Hardcover.

About the Author

S. Usher Evans was born and raised in Pensacola, Florida. After a decade of fighting bureaucratic battles as an IT consultant in Washington, DC, she suffered a massive quarter-life-crisis. She found fighting dragons was more fun than writing policy, so she moved back to Pensacola to write books full-time. She currently resides there with her husband and kids, and frequently can be found plotting on the beach.

Visit S. Usher Evans online at:
http://www.susherevans.com/